At Long Last, Love

A Collection

JUDY BAGSHAW

Pearlsong Press
Nashville, TN

© 2002, 2007 by Judy Bagshaw

Pearlsong Press
P.O. Box 58065
Nashville, TN 37205
www.pearlsong.com
www.pearlsongpress.com

ISBN: 9781597190084
Library of Congress Control Number: 2007924685

"Chance Encounter" was originally published in 2002 in SIGNATURES, an anthology by the Writer's Circle of Durham Region, Ontario, Canada. "Belle's Jingle" was originally published in the November 2002 issue of *Wynterblue Thunder* (now called *Wt-Blue Sky Region*) a literary journal out of Northern Ontario, Canada. "Saint Nic" was originally published on the *Wynterblue Thunder* website in 2001. "Duet," "Coming Home," "Always the Bridesmaid," and "Blue Collar Knight" were originally published as an ebook short collection by Shortstuff Books in 2002.

The *At Long Last, Love* collection minus "Chance Encounter" was originally published in trade paperback in 2004 by New Age Dimensions. The New Age Dimensions ebook version of *At Long Last, Love* contained only the first seven stories.

For my mother, who continues to inspire me.

Contents

Author's Note

*W*elcome to the shiny new edition of *At Long Last, Love,* my collection of short stories featuring big beautiful—and in some cases slightly more mature—heroines. Along with the new publisher and the new cover, this edition includes another story, making an even dozen romantic tales for your enjoyment.

These are heroines you'll recognize because they are real women like you and me. They have busy lives and character flaws. They make mistakes and have regrets. They long for love and have suffered hurts. But they persevere. And in the stories in this collection they find the love they've been looking for, sometimes where they least expect it.

As a reader myself, I was frustrated for years by the lack of stories that reflected the reality of my physical existence. I knew from experience that romance didn't have a dress size, so why wasn't I seeing full-figured women represented in popular romantic fiction? I decided to address that lack, and this collection is part of the result.

I hope you enjoy each and every story.

Judy Bagshaw

Duet

"*I* think he likes you." Tricia's face was a study of annoyance at her sister Mary's teasing words.

"Keep your voice down!" It was close to midnight, and many of the other passengers on the luxury tour bus were sleeping. Harry, their driver, had muted the lights, and a peaceful hush lay over the vehicle.

"Oh, stop being so prim," Mary said to her slightly older sibling. "He may look a little like the Pillsbury Dough Boy, but he's really kind of cute."

"I'm not playing this game with you," Tricia said, a smile threatening at the corner of her mouth. It was hard to resist Mary's inherent good humor. "I'm fifty-six years old, for heaven's sake. I don't even *use* the word cute where men are concerned. Besides, I'm a widow, remember?"

"Ben has been gone for two years now," Mary said, suddenly serious. "He would be the last person to want you to just sit yourself on a shelf. So, when I say I think Harry likes you, you're free to say, 'oh-really-how-nice-I rather-like-him-myself.'"

"Mary!" Tricia fixed a no-nonsense look on her face and glared at her sister.

"And that schoolmarm look of yours doesn't work, either,"

Mary said. "I've known you too long and I'm immune. Now, when are you going to speak to the man and put him out of his misery?"

Tricia chuckled in spite of her annoyance. Mary was incorrigible. "Probably at the same time you mind your own business and start acting your age!"

Mary feigned a thoughtful expression. "I could do that," she said. "Mind you, I don't feel my age. How do fifty-four-year-olds act anyhow?"

"Certainly not like starry-eyed fourteen-year-olds," Tricia said, taking her turn to tease her little sister. "Look, Mare, I agreed to come on this trip with you to relax and get away from things for a while. I'm not interested in romance. I had the great love of my life with Ben, and I'm content with those memories."

"Who are you trying to convince, me or you?" Mary said softly.

Tricia looked at her sister and felt exasperated. This was an old argument, one they'd been having for a year now. Mary thought Tricia was too young to just dry up and be the grieving widow for the rest of her life. But Mary didn't understand. Mary still had Bill. And their two boys had dutifully married nice girls and produced a grandbaby each. Tricia and Ben, as much as they had wanted a family, had never had children. Memories were all Tricia had to hold on to. So she was reluctant to let them go.

She smiled with great affection at her sister. "Get some sleep, Mare," she said gently. "We'll be at the hotel soon. Tomorrow will be a big day."

"You can't avoid this conversation forever," Mary said, putting her seat back and getting comfortable.

"I can certainly try," Tricia said, doing the same.

"RISE AND SHINE," Harry said in his jovial, deep voice. A look in his mirror showed most of the passengers shifting to a seated position and groggily trying to pull themselves together.

He particularly noticed the classy redhead five rows back, and he sighed to himself. Even just emerging from sleep, she was lovely.

If only he—

"Hey, Harry!" Suzy, the tour guide, had suddenly appeared at his shoulder.

"What's up, kiddo?" he said to the perky, freckle-faced girl.

"Where were you just now?" she said.

"What do you mean?"

"I had to say your name three times before you answered."

He felt his face go hot and knew he must be blushing. Suzy began to giggle. "Why the blush?" And then her eyes grew wide with amusement. "Okay, who is she?"

"Oh, cut it out," Harry said, trying to sound severe.

"Let's see if I can guess." She stood and faced the passengers, craning to see faces. "I don't think it's Betty Shneider. She's a little too gossipy, I think, for your taste."

"I said cut it out," Harry said, hoping like mad no one could hear Suzy's teasing speculations. He was by nature a very shy man and really didn't like this kind of attention.

"Connie, Barbara and Greta are all with their hubbies," Suzy remarked thoughtfully, "unless there's an unscrupulous side of you I don't know."

"I won't even dignify that remark," Harry said. "Now come on. Be a good girl and sit back down."

"In a minute. Let's see. Shirley—No. Maude—Definitely not. —Wait! I know!"

Harry cringed.

"It's that nice Mrs. Martin—Tricia!"

Harry's blush deepened and he could feel his stomach tense. He answered as calmly as he could. "Suzy, you have a wild imagination. Now, have you called the hotel to make sure they're expecting us? We'll be there in less than twenty minutes."

"Oh, cripes, thanks for reminding me," Suzy said, and dug for her cell phone.

Having effectively distracted her, Harry took a deep, calming breath and focused on his driving. It bothered him that Suzy had come so close to guessing his secret.

He had indeed noticed Mrs. Martin—Tricia—from the moment she had first boarded the bus two days ago. She was so elegant, so gracious. She had smiled at him and been so nice that Harry had felt he was on top of the world. He'd even written a song about her, not that he'd ever tell her that.

"Okay, all set," Suzy chirped in his ear. "So was I right?"

Harry cringed inside. *Here we go again.* "You have a one-track mind, little girl," he said gruffly. "How about you leave the old man alone and take care of your passengers."

Suzy laughed and patted Harry on the shoulder. "Okay, I'll drop it for now," she said with affection. "But I'm not going to give up playing matchmaker here. I give you fair warning."

Heaven help me, Harry thought.

Harry had been a bachelor his whole life. Oh, he'd had his small share of romances over the years, but he'd never made it to the altar. His four sisters had made it their business to try and find him a nice wife. But he was mostly just embarrassed by their fix-ups and the enforced dinner dates. He didn't know why. He supposed it was because he was such a backward sort with women, shy and unsure of himself—which was strange since he'd grown up in a house full of women. But he never knew what to say and was always conscious of his balding head and soft paunch.

He told himself he was happy with his single life. He loved his job and got to travel and meet lots of wonderful people. But if he looked deep inside himself, he had to admit he was lonely. He'd have to retire sometime in the next few years, and the prospect of living the rest of his days alone was terrifying to him.

He pulled into the hotel parking lot. "Here we are folks," he announced on the intercom. "Enjoy the next two days."

"I HOPE YOU ENJOYED your excursion to the beach today," Suzy said, her entire persona exuding youth and energy. The crowd applauded enthusiastically. "Great! Tomorrow we have a bus arranged for the morning's shopping excursion and, for those interested, you can sign up for the sightseeing tour in the afternoon. The rest of you who shop till you drop can stay here and nap poolside." Laughter filled the room.

"Were we ever this perky?" Mary murmured for Tricia's ears only.

"No one's this perky!" Tricia said.

"And now for a little surprise," Suzy continued, "you all know Harry, our driver." The group clapped and cheered, for Harry had quickly endeared himself to his passengers with his quiet friendliness and willingness to help. "What you might not know is that our beloved Harry is a wonderful singer and guitar player."

There was a murmur of surprised interest.

"Now, it took quite a bit of persuading and you'll have to help me get him up here, but Harry has agreed to provide a little after-dinner entertainment for us. So, before he loses his nerve—"

A ripple of laughter ran through the room.

"—let's have a round of applause for Harry 'The Singing Bus Driver' Davenport!"

A red-faced but smiling Harry ambled up to the front and perched on a stool.

"Well, well, well," Mary said in an amused drawl. "Still waters do run deep, don't they?"

"What?" Tricia was watching as Harry checked his tuning and tested the microphone.

"Harry," Mary said, noting the interest her sister was taking in the front of the room. "Who would have figured him for a trou-badour?"

"What's so strange about that?" Tricia turned to look at Mary.

"Oh, nothing, I suppose," Mary said with mock nonchalance. "But it got me thinking."

"Oh-oh," Tricia moaned.

"Well, you and Harry have this in common, don't you? You were a music teacher and you belonged to that barbershop group for—how many years?"

"More than I care to remember," Tricia replied.

"And look at all those trophies you got for singing."

"Mary, that was in grade school, for heaven's sake." Tricia shook her head. "Now be quiet. I want to hear Harry."

"I'm sure you do," Mary muttered, not sure Tricia had caught the remark until she felt her sister's elbow in her ribs. She smiled smugly.

"Well—um—I feel a little silly sitting up here," Harry said. He scratched behind his ear nervously. "I think Suzy got a little over-enthused." The crowd chuckled in understanding. "I hope you won't be disappointed. So, here goes nothin'."

The lights were dimmed. Harry sat in the spot, hunkered over the guitar. His eyes closed and the crowd hushed in expectation. They weren't disappointed.

Harry's rich, deep baritone delivered the first few words of an old country love song and the audience was enraptured.

"Wow," Mary said in awe.

Tricia was speechless. Music had been her whole life, hers and Ben's. Music had brought them together, and music had been a huge focus in their home. It was through music that Tricia was able to express herself best. It was music that helped her deal with Ben's death and helped her keep her precious memories intact.

Now she found herself shaken to the very core. Harry's voice was rich and vibrant. It was obvious he loved music as much as she did. He played the guitar almost lovingly, and she was sure he was totally oblivious to the audience now. All that existed was the song.

It was a sad ballad of love found and then lost, broken hearts and broken dreams, and Harry sang as if he understood personally each word the composer had written. Tricia felt tears begin to course down her cheeks, but she ignored them. She sat motionless, drinking in the warmth of Harry's voice.

She was startled by the eruption of applause that began a few beats after Harry finished. Most of the people had jumped to their feet, paying tribute to a wonderful performer. Tricia sat demolished by the emotions his singing had evoked.

"Are you all right, Trish?" Mary put her hand on Tricia's arm, concerned by the tears Tricia was only now beginning to wipe dry.

"That was wonderful," Tricia said with a sigh. "Wasn't that wonderful?" She gripped Mary's hand with her own.

"He can sing, that's for sure," Mary said.

"That wasn't just singing," Tricia said fiercely. "That was—that was—"

"Well, well, well," Mary said, sitting back with a grin. "Looks like big sister has been bitten by the 'love bug.'" She said the final words with an exaggerated drawl, her eyebrows twitching up and down for emphasis.

"Oh, don't be ridiculous," Tricia said angrily. She blew her nose. "Can I not just enjoy a really good performance without you making it into some kind of juvenile love story?"

"Hmmm," Mary said, not the least put off by Tricia's anger. "Methinks she doth protest too much."

"Oh, for heaven's sake! Grow up and stop all this nonsense!"

"What nonsense?" Both women jumped at Harry's sudden presence at their table.

"Well, I was just telling my sister here—" Mary began.

"Nothing!" Tricia said forcefully. "My 'baby' sister sometimes forgets she's a middle-aged woman."

"And Tricia feels the need to remind me," Mary said wryly.

Harry chuckled and sat down.

"I guess that's what comes with having siblings," he said. "I just came to see if you were all right." This directed at Tricia. "Suzy said you looked upset when I was singing."

"Oh dear," Tricia said, embarrassed. "No, I wasn't upset. I was completely overwhelmed by your singing. You have a wonderful voice. I hope you're going to sing some more for us."

"My sister's a musician, too," Mary piped in.

"Really?" Harry was pleasantly surprised.

"Oh, I don't know if musician is the right word," Tricia said softly.

"Nonsense," Mary said. "She has a great voice, and she plays piano. She and Ben were barber-shoppers."

Harry's heart dropped. "Ben?"

"My late husband."

Harry's heart leapt. Silently he chastised himself for being glad at this news. "I'm sorry," was all he could find to say.

"Maybe Trish could sing with you," Mary suggested.

"Mary!" Now Tricia was truly embarrassed. She could kill Mary for her meddling. Not that she wasn't tempted. Her contralto would blend nicely with Harry's baritone. She could harmonize easily. It would be nice to sing with a man again, and Harry was such a nice man. She blushed and wondered why she did.

"Pay no attention to Mary's ramblings," she said, trying to make light of the disastrous turn of the conversation. "Please. Favor us with another song, will you?"

"I'd be delighted," Harry said. "Any requests? I have quite a repertoire."

"Oh, let's see—"

"Wait," Harry said as he stood to leave. "I think I have just the song. I hope you like it."

The two women watched Harry return to his makeshift stage.

"I'm positive he has a thing for you," Mary said, grinning at her sister.

"What?" Tricia blushed crimson. "Don't be silly. He's just a nice, kind man." But she watched intently as Harry prepared to sing. Mary's speculation, instead of making her angry, had given her food for thought.

"I'm just saying that I think with a little encouragement—"

"You just won't stop, will you?" Tricia said. "I told you I'm not interested."

"Aren't you? You're sure about that."

"Of course, I'm sure. I'm too old to be looking for romance anyway. I told you I'm quite happy with my life as it is."

"Go ahead. Keep telling yourself that. You might even actually believe it one day. And fifty-six is not old, okay? You have a lot of living yet to do. Wouldn't it be wonderful to find someone to share that time with?"

Tricia chose to ignore her sister. If she looked closely at the true source of her irritation, it was that Mary was hitting too close to the truth, and it rattled her. She didn't want to be rattled.

She had finally accepted Ben's death and had settled into a comfortable routine. She didn't need to have that all mixed up again. Or did she? She shifted restlessly in her seat, wishing the whole subject would just go away.

The crowd hushed and Tricia sat up, ready for Harry's next song. When it came, she was devastated. Why *that* song? Why *now?*

"Are the stars out tonight?" Harry crooned the old standard.

Tricia's throat felt tight as the familiar and devastating lyrics washed over her.

"Gee, I wonder why he chose *that* particular song?" Mary teased. But her humor drained when she saw the look on Tricia's face. "Trish?"

Tricia felt Harry's eyes on her, but her own were filled with tears. She stumbled to her feet.

"Trish, for God's sake," Mary said, and reached for her sister's hand. "What's wrong?"

Tricia didn't hear. Her ears buzzed and a sob rose in her throat. He couldn't have known. It was just an awful coincidence. Tears welled in her eyes and she knew she was about to make a complete spectacle of herself, and that she wouldn't do. Without a word to her rather startled sister, she grabbed her bag and fled the room, keeping her head down and a hand over her mouth.

SHE WAS SURE she didn't breathe until the door to her room had closed behind her. A wrenching sob tore from her throat and she gave vent to the flood of tears. Mary found her lying on her bed curled in a ball, weeping openly.

"Oh my God, Trish!" Mary sat gingerly on the edge of the bed and stroked her sister's back and shoulders. "What is it, honey?"

"Th-th-that song," Tricia said weakly. "That's *our* song."

"Yours and Ben's," Mary said as understanding dawned. "You poor thing. What can I get you? How about some tea?" And she rose to get it.

They sat against the headboard, their hands wrapped around the mugs of steaming brew. Hot tears had ravaged Tricia's face and she sniffed softly, but the worst of the storm seemed to have passed.

"It just hit me so hard," she said, her voice wobbly with emotion. "Ben sang 'I Only Have Eyes for You' to me the night he first told me he loved me. I'll never forget it. We were so young. We'd gone to a country club dance and we sneaked out to the patio and were dancing under the stars in the moonlight. It was so incredibly romantic. The band struck up that song. He took me in his arms and said, 'I love you, Trish,' and then he sang along with the band."

"I remember," Mary said with a smile. "You came home walking on air. You looked so happy. I think the whole family knew then that Ben would become a part of the family."

"And he sang it to me at every anniversary."

"He was a sappy romantic, for sure."

"He was such a wonderful husband, Mary." Tears welled again in Tricia's eyes. "I miss him so much."

"I know you do, honey. I know."

"But—"

Mary looked at her sister. "But?"

"I think I've been lying to myself about being so content with my life. I don't feel like a middle-aged woman. I feel young and vital and I miss the feel of a man's arms around me and the intimacy of sharing a life with someone. I loved Ben with all my heart, but lately—"

"What?"

"Well, I find myself feeling—lonely. And I know it's stupid, but I feel guilty, as if I'm betraying Ben's memory."

"Ben would want you to be happy again, Trish, you know that."

"I think I do, Sis. Whew! I bet you didn't anticipate any of this when you suggested this trip." Tricia gave a weak laugh.

"Hey, what are little sisters for?"

"Annoying their big sisters?"

"Hey!" Mary was about to hit Tricia with a pillow when they heard a knock on the door. Mary opened the door to find a worried-looking Harry.

"Is Mrs. Martin—Tricia, all right? I saw her run from the lounge and then, when you followed, I was worried she might be sick or something."

Mary smiled.

"I'm afraid she had an attack of acute nostalgia."

"I beg your pardon?"

"The song you sang was hers and her husband's special song."

"Oh my, I'm so sorry." Harry was stricken. "I didn't—I'd never—I hope she'll forgive me."

"There's nothing to forgive," Tricia said. "Mary, let the poor man in the door."

Tricia had managed to straighten herself and looked quite composed standing by the balcony window.

"Hi, Harry," she said with a valiant attempt at a bright smile.

"I'm sorry I upset you," Harry said.

"It wasn't you, Harry," said Tricia, coming forward to take Harry's hand in hers. "Your singing was wonderful, truly wonderful, and I enjoyed it so much. It's a gift to move someone so greatly with music. As Mary said, in her inimitable way, I had an attack of nostalgia. It's past now. I want to thank you for being so kind and checking up on me."

"I—well—it was nothing." Harry was suddenly flushed and uncomfortable. "I just wanted to make sure you—both of you—were all right. I should go now. Have a nice night now, ladies, and—um—don't forget, the bus leaves early tomorrow for the shopping district."

Mary chuckled at Harry's hasty retreat.

"My, my, my," she said. The pillow hit her squarely on the back of the head.

TRICIA AND MARY hurried toward the bus the next morning.

"Oh, we're going to be late," Tricia said crossly. "I hate being late. Why did you have to take so long to decide what to wear?"

"Stop being so grouchy," Mary snapped back. "Just because you're in a rotten mood doesn't mean the rest of world has to be, too."

"I'm not in a rotten mood. I just don't like to be late and keep everyone waiting. It's rude and inconsiderate."

"Oh, so now I'm rude and inconsiderate. Thanks so much."

"Stop twisting my words. You know what I meant."

"Sure. You meant that it's my fault that we're late."

"I didn't say—" Tricia stopped and grabbed Mary's arm, stopping her, too. "For heaven's sake, listen to us. We sound like a couple of eight-year-olds. I'm sorry, Mare. I didn't sleep too well and I'm out of sorts."

Mary smiled and patted her sister's hand.

"I'm sorry, too. Are you still upset about last night?"

"Yes, I guess I am," Tricia replied. "But not about what you might think."

"Oh?"

"I've been thinking about Harry."

Mary grinned. "Oh?"

"Stop it," Tricia said with a chuckle, and she playfully slapped Mary's arm. "I meant that I think I may have somehow upset Harry."

"Really? I didn't think so. He seemed to be genuinely concerned."

"Yes, I agree. He was being kind. But when I mentioned that his song reminded me of Ben—well, don't you think he beat a pretty hasty retreat?"

Mary paused a moment and thought. "Looking at it like that, I suppose he did. Maybe he just felt uncomfortable. He's a pretty shy man."

"Maybe." Tricia glanced at the waiting bus. "Oh gosh, look. Everyone has boarded already. There's Suzy waiting. This is so embarrassing." The two women hurried toward the now frantically waving girl.

"We just about gave up on you," Suzy said with a grin. "In fact, I said to Harry that you'd probably decided to spend the day sunbathing."

"Not us," Mary quipped. "We're a couple of shopping fools. Lead us to our financial doom, Suzy!"

A ripple of laughter went through the bus.

"Good morning, Harry," Tricia said softly, pausing by the

driver's seat.

"Good morning—uh—Mrs. Martin," Harry said, only glancing briefly her way and looking quite interested in the contents of his clipboard.

"Tricia, please."

Harry looked at her sadly. "Tricia."

"Harry, I was hoping we could—"

"We're ready to go, Mrs. Martin," Suzy said brightly, "as soon as you're in your seat."

With a final, pointed look at Harry, Tricia made her way to her seat.

"What was that all about?" Suzy asked quietly.

"Oh, be quiet!" Harry snapped and angrily put the bus into gear. Suzy was startled into silence.

"What did Harry have to say?" Mary asked with feigned innocence. Tricia was not fooled.

"Very little, I'm afraid. I really think he's quite upset. It's like he's withdrawn into himself. I tried—oh, never mind. He's not interested, and that's that."

"How can two grown people be so obtuse?" Mary said, shaking her head with exasperation.

"What souvenirs are you going to get the kids?" The subject firmly changed, the two women concentrated on enjoying their excursion.

An idea began to form in Tricia's mind and had become fully realized by the time they returned to the hotel.

"I'm not going on the sightseeing tour this afternoon," she told Mary.

"Oh? Well, then, why don't we just put on our suits and make use of that beautiful pool, or maybe go sit a while by the seawall and watch the waves?"

"Um, I think you should go with the group. Enjoy yourself. I'll just rest and read my book. I, uh, need some quiet time."

"Uh-huh." Mary began to glimpse Tricia's strategy. "Harry's not driving this afternoon, is he?"

"Gee, I guess not. I think it's a local tour company." Tricia spoke lightly, sounding unconcerned.

"Uh-huh. I suppose he needs some quiet time too, to maybe read a book."

"Maybe." Tricia was suddenly intent on sorting through her purchases.

"Uh-huh. Well, I'll just go to the front desk and make sure I'm signed up."

"That's a good idea. Have fun this afternoon."

"Sure, and good luck when you talk to Harry." Mary laughed at Tricia's startled expression. Then she smiled with genuine sisterly support. "I really do hope it goes well."

"Thanks, Mare."

"HI, HARRY." Tricia found Harry sitting alone on a park bench near the sea wall, strumming his guitar idly and staring at the waves. He jumped at the sound of her voice.

"Hi," he said. He stood quickly and looked unsure.

Tricia was filled with a sense of protectiveness toward the man. "I'm sorry to disturb you," she said.

"You're not," he said, turning red. "I mean, I wasn't doing anything important."

"Just relaxing, I guess."

"Yeah. Tomorrow will be a long day of driving."

"It's hard to believe the trip is almost over."

"Time flies."

An awkward silence descended. Tricia's gaze connected with Harry's and she tried to convey reassurance to him with a smile. It seemed he understood, because he soon smiled shyly himself.

"Would you like to sit down?" he asked, indicating the bench.

"I was hoping we could talk a bit," Tricia said as she took her place. Harry sat and leaned his guitar against the bench's arm. With some trepidation he angled himself to look at Tricia. She sat primly, staring at her clenched hands.

"I want to explain a few things," she began, her voice soft and containing a nervous quaver. "My husband, Ben, died two years ago. Heart attack. We never saw it coming and it was the worst shock. I went from a blissfully happy marriage to sudden widow-hood, and I think I really fell apart for a while. Mary and her family were wonderful, and my own mother was a great help since she too was a widow, and slowly, over that first year, I recovered and began to live again.

"I dropped any of the activities Ben and I had done as a cou-ple—mostly music and theatre things—and concentrated on my last year as a music teacher. I retired this spring, and Mary sug-gested this trip.

"I guess what I'm trying to say is that I thought I had created a nice, quiet, comfortable, solo life for myself and that I was truly happy and content. But Mary is a great one for getting you to examine your illusions closely." She said this with an affectionate smile. "And in looking at things closely, I realized that I was fool-ing myself. I've been lonely and unhappy and didn't want to accept it."

Harry had listened intently. He patted her arm. "Don't be hard on yourself. We all delude ourselves from time to time. I think it's a way of protecting ourselves from hurt."

"You sound like you understand."

"Believe me, I do." He sounded bitter.

"Last night, when you sang our song—"

"I'm so sorry—"

"No, it's all right. When you sang our song, it just made me realize that it's not so much Ben anymore that I miss, although I do—it's the *togetherness*, the sharing that I miss more. I see now that I have a lot of my life ahead of me, and I don't necessarily want to go through it alone."

"I know what you mean," Harry said, again staring out to the water. "I retire in the next couple of years, and I've been thinking the same things."

"You never married?"

"Nah. I just never met the right—No, that's not quite true." He turned to look at Tricia. "I'm a real shy person, but I guess you noticed that. And I'm no movie star to look at. I guess that combination just made it harder to find Ms. Right."

"I think you're a very nice man," Tricia said.

Harry smiled and blushed. "Thank you. But nice only gets you so far in the romance department, I've found. I seem to always become the guy friend who ladies tell about their heartbreaks with the good-looking guys they still care about."

"Niceness and kindness are wonderful qualities. My husband had them both."

"And he was good-looking, too, I'll bet."

"Actually, he was built a lot like you, maybe a little taller, and his hair was darker. I called him my teddy bear."

"Really?" Harry was taken by surprise. It had never occurred to him that Tricia might actually find someone like him attractive. He found he was thrilled at the notion. "I just assumed—"

"I thought he was very handsome," she said with a shy smile. "But it was the goodness of his heart and soul that really won my heart in the end. And the fact that he was a hopeless romantic."

"It sounds like you had a wonderful marriage."

"We did."

"He was a lucky man."

"I was a lucky woman."

The two fell silent, each knowing they were on the brink of something momentous and both afraid of saying or doing something that would break the delicate thread between them. So they just sat looking at the waves breaking on the shore.

Several moments passed, and Tricia was aware of how perfectly content she felt sitting at Harry's side. A quiet peacefulness filled her and she realized that for the first time in a long time, Ben was not foremost in her thoughts. Instead she was thinking of how lovely it was to share the time and the view with such a sweet man as Harry.

Harry was also aware of how content he was feeling, and comfortable. His shyness seemed to have vanished in the face of Tricia's quiet acceptance of him as a person.

As though driven by the same impulse, the two reached out a hand. When their fingers touched, a subtle change came over the atmosphere around them. Everything seemed a little clearer and brighter.

They looked into each other's eyes, smiled, and wove their fingers together.

"YOU WOULD NOT BELIEVE how annoying that Barbara Anderson and her obnoxious husband are. With you not there, I was stuck with them for the afternoon. If I hear one more chorus of 'Our son Michael is just sooooo wonderful' I'll throw up!" Mary threw her bag on the bed and proceeded angrily to change from her dusty, wrinkled clothes. "I tried to ditch them at the butterfly museum, but they managed to find me again. These people just don't take a hint! I was ready to throttle the woman!"

"That's nice," Tricia said. She sat on the balcony, staring out over the water, a bemused expression on her face.

Mary came to the door and stared at her sister. A slow smile spread over her face. "So I told the woman that her precious Michael was no doubt a paragon of virtue, but could he play the drums while standing on his head whistling Dixie?"

"Uh-huh?" Tricia said.

"Trish?"

"Yes?"

"What did I just say?"

"What?"

"Just now, what did I just say?"

Tricia turned a puzzled face to Mary. "What do you mean?"

Mary laughed and wagged her finger at her sister. "As soon as I'm out of the shower, you will tell me what went on today with Harry. Although by the beatific smile on your face, I'd say that all is well and *I* was right!"

Tricia grinned. "Could be!"

"Woo-hoo!" Mary shouted as she went into the bathroom.

DINNER SEEMED to drag. Harry was nowhere in sight, and Tricia was concerned that maybe she had misinterpreted the afternoon.

"Don't be silly," Mary said. "He's maybe busy getting things ready to start the return trip—paperwork and stuff."

"You think so?"

"I think so. Now stop fretting and enjoy this wonderful dinner, and tonight we splurge on a really wicked dessert. What do you say?"

"Hmm?"

"Honestly," Mary laughed. "I hope he's not as absent-minded as you are. I don't think I'd trust his driving."

"Oh, stop it!" Tricia blushed and focused on her meal.

Finally dinner was over and the tables cleared. Some of the tour members ambled off to early bed, but most stayed for one last night of entertainment and fun. Tricia was too wound up to feel sleepy. Harry had still not made an appearance.

Mary kept reassuring her sister that all was well, but she was beginning to have doubts, too. She would never forgive herself if her meddling caused Tricia another broken heart.

"Look, there's Suzy. I'll go ask her where Harry is," Mary said.

But that wasn't needed, for Harry entered behind Suzy, carrying his guitar, a broad grin on his face attesting to his wellbeing.

Suzy stepped up to the mike as Harry took his place on the small stage.

"We have a very special treat for you tonight," she said with her usual vivacious delivery. The crowd cheered. Suzy waved them quiet. "Harry has offered to play one of his own compositions for you tonight!" Another round of cheers and applause filled the air. Suzy's eyes twinkled. "And I'm to tell you that this is dedicated to a special someone—"

Tricia was alarmed to see so many heads turn in her direction. Mary elbowed her. "Seems like the proverbial cat is out of the bag."

"Shhhh!" Tricia squirmed in her seat, but managed a wan smile at Harry.

" —and he's calling the song 'Duet.'"

The lights were dimmed and an air of expectancy draped the room. Harry finished tuning and, with a subtle wink in Tricia's direction, began to sing.

*"I'm a singer singing solo, looking for some harmony.
But I never seemed to find it.
Where's the one who's meant for me?"*

Various members of the crowd were shouting suggestions and being quickly hushed by spouses.

*"So imagine what it felt like when you walked into the room.
And I felt my heartstrings quiver, with a sentimental tune."*

"Oh my God," Mary said, grabbing Tricia's arm. "He's singing about you."

Tricia's face felt hot and her heart beat rapidly in her chest. She was thrilled and embarrassed in equal measure. Tears welled in her eyes, but she quickly rubbed them aside. Harry's warm, deep voice washed over her in welcome waves.

*"You are the one I've searched for.
I knew it when we met.
This is the start of something new.
I hope you've felt this feeling too.
I bless the day that I found you—
we make a nice duet."*

Harry stopped and paused, his head bent over his guitar. Then an explosion of applause erupted and he found himself standing and walking toward Tricia's table, using the applause to fuel his courage.

Tricia watched him approach and knew her legs were too weak to support her if she stood. But as he took her hand in his, strength filled her and she stood to face him. They gazed intently into each other's eyes, no words needed. And in that moment, both felt the mantle of loneliness lift.

They didn't even hear the roar of approval from the crowd or Mary's exclaimed "Finally!" as their lips met in their first kiss.

Coming Home

Tears filled Bev Randall's eyes as she pulled into the driveway of her childhood home. It had been twenty years. Her parents were gone now, both victims of cancer. Lorraine, Bev's older sister, lived here now with her family. It was Lorraine who carried on the family business, Wexford's, the lumberyard that had been their father's obsession and the unwitting reason for Bev's banishment. Memories flooded her mind.

It was at the lumberyard, her senior year in high school, that she met Jim Randall, a sexy rebel in tight blue jeans. He convinced her to dump Darren, her steady, and charmed his way into taking her virginity, forever altering the course of her life. She had so foolishly run away with him. Unknown to her, he had also run off with the payroll from the lumberyard. Once she had found that out, it was too late to explain her ignorance to her parents.

Bev shook her head. No good rehashing all that spilled milk. She looked up and was startled to see Lorraine standing on the front porch, arms crossed, just watching Bev sitting in her car. How long had she been there? Oh, well, no avoiding it now.

Bev slowly got out of the car, her heart beating rapidly as panic threatened to seize her. "Hello, Lorraine," she said softly from the safety of the driveway.

"I wondered if you were ever going to get out," Lorraine said, a smile sprouting on her face. "Welcome home."

With those simple words, Bev's fear vanished. The two sisters flew into each other's arms and the twenty-year gap was bridged.

SITTING IN THE COZY WARMTH of the old house's kitchen, Bev was yanked back to the past.

Her father had been in a towering rage. Her mother had wept and pleaded for her eldest, her precious child with so much promise, to see reason. Lorraine was out on a date and would hear the sad story later. Who knows? Had Lorraine been there, she might have been the one to turn the tide of Bev's decision.

"I love him," Bev had cried with all the conviction her teenage heart could muster. "And he loves me. He says we can get married!"

"Married," her father thundered. "You could have thought of that before you got knocked up!"

"Ted, please!" her mother pleaded. "Don't talk like that. Beverly, he didn't mean it. He's upset."

"I damn well did mean it," Ted Wexford roared.

Never in all her life had Bev seen her father spit such venom. She was terrified. "I didn't mean to get pregnant," she sobbed, her own anger and frustration building. "We love each other."

"You were raised in a respectable home!" her father ranted. "You were not raised to take up with some lowlife, two-faced, hustler con-artist like Jim Randall. So help me, if I get my hands on him—"

"I love him!" Bev screamed. "Can't you get that? I love him. We want to get married and raise our baby!"

"Not as long as I live!" her father roared. Her mother sobbed.

"We don't need your permission," Bev dared.

"As long as you live in this house, you do!"

"Then I'll leave!" she countered.

Her mother had uttered a grief-filled "No!" but the fateful step had been taken.

Bev stormed out of the house and found Jimmy at his rooming house. With nothing but their love to sustain them—or so Bev had thought—they had ridden out of town in Jim's pickup truck. Three days later she learned what Jim had done and was horrified. But by then, she was Mrs. Jim Randall, for better or worse, and she left her childhood behind.

"Things haven't changed much," Bev said now, surveying the kitchen. "I was just thinking about the last time I was in this room."

Lorraine placed steaming mugs of coffee on the table and sat across from her. "In some ways, I'm glad I wasn't here for that," she said. "But I felt terrible that I didn't get to say good-bye."

"Dad was so awful," Bev said, absently stirring her coffee. "I guess pride got in both our ways. And by the time Jimmy and I were married and I discovered he'd stolen the money from the lumberyard, I figured it was all too late."

"It must have been terrible for you," Lorraine said.

"It was. I was so stupid to think that I was in love with Jim or he, truly, with me."

"Everyone's stupid at 17."

"I guess, but I think I took it to a whole new level." Bev sipped her coffee and sighed. "This tastes so good. The kids and I have been traveling for three days. I was ready to kill for a good cup of coffee."

"Why didn't you bring the kids with you?"

"I wanted to make this first visit home on my own. I figured I'd be pretty emotional. I was right. They're just at the motel, probably at each other's throats by now."

"I'm glad you finally wrote to me." Lorraine stood to fetch a box of chocolate wafers from the counter. "Brad was what, six? Seven?"

"Seven. Jimmy had just gone to jail the first time." An embarassed silence descended on the two women for a moment. "I needed a shoulder to cry on."

"God, Bev, how awful it must have been."

Bev's eyes spoke volumes about the disappointments that had

filled her married life. "It was. Oh, I knew by then that he was no good, but I had a seven-year-old and Christy was four. I felt I had nowhere else to go. So I got work waitressing and we somehow managed. Jimmy got out and I stupidly ended up pregnant again. Not that I'm not glad I have Teddy. He's the light of my life—a real charmer."

She chuckled and then sobered again. "But it kept me even more tied." She got thoughtful for a moment. "I can't believe my first-born is away at university. Time sure does fly."

"It does that! You could have come home, Bev," Lorraine said. "I told you that Dad regretted his words in the end. They would have loved to have met the kids."

"Don't you see, Lo? I was so ashamed. Too much water had gone under the bridge. I didn't believe they could forgive me. I suppose because I couldn't forgive myself."

"Why didn't you come for the funerals?" Lorraine said, showing a sudden interest in the crumbs on the tablecloth.

"Jimmy got work in Alaska," Bev said. "We were just scraping by. We just didn't have the money for me to make the trip."

"What about after you divorced him?"

"Well, I took the kids and left Alaska. We went back east and I got a job waiting tables. It was a struggle at first, but somehow we got by, got a little house. Bradley was wonderful. He was just twelve or thirteen, but he had paper routes and odd jobs and just had a flair for making money. And he'd contribute to the family coffers. Christy baby-sat, worked at burger joints. But when you sent me the information about the school reunion, it just suddenly hit me how much I wanted to come back."

"Well, you're here now," Lorraine said to lighten the mood. "I insist you fetch the kids and your luggage and stay here."

"Are you sure there's room?"

"Sure, I'm sure. Gary and the kids will be thrilled."

Gary may have been pleased to finally meet his sister-in-law, but seventeen-year-old Tyler and twelve-year-old Faye were wary at the invasion. Christy's response to her cousins' coolness was to adopt a dismissive air of her own, as only a sixteen-year-old can do. Teddy was like a big happy puppy. He liked everyone, sure that everyone liked him equally well.

Things seemed to thaw a bit by dinnertime, and the whole family chattered and exchanged information freely.

"You'll never guess who I ran into today when I went to get groceries," Lorraine said to Bev.

"Probably not," Bev said. "I haven't been here for a while."

"Darren McKenny!"

Bev froze with a forkful of lasagna halfway to her mouth. Her face lost its color and her eyes went wide with shock.

Lorraine seemed not to notice her sister's discomfort. "He got a job here after he got married, teaching English at the high school. Say, Ty, doesn't he teach you English this year?"

"Nah, I had him last year. I liked him okay."

"He's going to be at the reunion. In fact, I think he was on the organizing committee—Bev? Are you all right?"

Bev stood unsteadily and pushed her chair back.

"If you'll just excuse me," she said weakly and left the room.

With a muttered "Damn," Lorraine went after her. She found Bev in the kitchen, head bowed, leaning heavily on the edge of the kitchen sink.

"Me and my big mouth," Lorraine said, touching Bev on the shoulder. Bev's shoulders heaved and a sob broke from her throat.

"I don't know where that came from," she said.

Lorraine handed her a tissue.

"I have always felt so awful about what I did to Darren then."

"Hey, you were young and naïve and got swept off your feet by a more experienced Jimmy. We all thought he was pretty cool, remember?"

"And I was so proud when he picked me." Bev looked at her sister sadly. "He was like no one I'd ever known before, certainly like no one in Beaverbrook. So exciting! Darren suddenly seemed so dull in comparison." She started to cry even more. "Oh, Lorraine, I hurt him so badly."

Lorraine's heart was breaking as she witnessed Bev's anguish. She pulled her younger sibling into her arms and stroked her back and rocked her. "I think he understood in the end, Bev."

Bev sniffed and pulled from Lorraine's embrace. "Tell me about him—his life. Was he happy?"

The two women sat at the kitchen table.

"Shortly after you and Jim left town, Darren went away to school. So I didn't see much of him for about four years. His parents stayed next door until Mr. McKenny had his heart attack and died. Mrs. McKenny didn't want to stay in the big house, and she sold it. She moved into the new condo complex they built in the north end of town, and she opened a cute little gift shop downtown that's done quite well.

"Darren met Cathy—that was his wife's name—at school, and they married shortly after graduating. She was a big shot lawyer's daughter from Chicago, I think. She wasn't too keen on moving to Beaverbrook —we're too small town for her city tastes—but it's where Darren could get a teaching job and where he wanted to live. I don't think they had a very happy marriage. She was restless and they didn't have any kids. Darren seemed to have become so withdrawn and gloomy all the time. One day she just up and took off, and that was the last we ever saw of her."

"Oh, poor Darren," Bev said. "He didn't deserve that. But then, he didn't deserve what I did to him either."

"He is kind of bitter, I guess," Lorraine said. "As far as I know he's never been serious with anyone else, and, quite frankly, not too many women go after him because he's so quiet and keeps to himself. It's like he's built this wall around himself."

Bev's eyes filled with tears again. "Look at all the pain I caused," she whispered.

Lorraine took Bev's hands in her own. "What's done is done," she said. "There is nothing to be gained by beating yourself up. You have finally taken control of your own life, and you have three wonderful kids. You need to start living in the now!"

"You're right, Lo," Bev said, giving her sister a wan smile.

"I often am!" Lorraine said, smiling back.

"Mom?" Christy stood in the doorway.

Bev patted the spot beside her at the table, and the sixteen-year-old ambled over. Bev put her arm around her daughter. "I'm okay, honey," she said. "Your Aunt Lorraine has just given me some sound advice. How would you feel if we stuck around Beaverbrook?"

"You mean for good?"

"Well, for a while anyway."

Christy pondered the question for a few moments and then nodded. "I think it's a good idea," she said. "We all need to make a fresh start."

Lorraine smiled." I couldn't have said it better myself."

IT AMAZED BEV how quickly she settled back into the rhythms of small town living. She had been so tense and miserable for so long that she had forgotten how good happy could be. Walking through town was like finally getting a good big breath of clean fresh air. Here she found all the happy memories that put to rest the regrets and misery of the past. Here, she knew she could begin again.

McKenny's Gift Shoppe was situated on the northeast corner of the central four-corners of the town. The window was filled with an intriguing selection of art and crafts. She was so intent on looking at all the lovely objects that she didn't notice at first when someone stopped beside her.

"Hello, Bev," he said, and Bev started. With a pounding heart, she looked up into the solemn, older face of Darren McKenny.

"Hello," was all she could manage to say.

"Lorraine said you were coming for the reunion."

"Yes. I'm here with two of my children."

The two looked at each other for a few moments, noting the subtle changes that had come with the passage of time.

"You haven't changed much," he said.

"Nor have you."

Awkwardness hung between them, making conversation difficult.

"Well," he said, "I guess I'll see you around."

"Yes, I guess."

And he was gone.

Bev stood rooted on the spot. Her heart hammered and her mouth had suddenly gone dry. She closed her eyes and saw his face again before her. In his eyes had been an echo of the hurt she had inflicted on him the day she broke off their relationship.

"Why, Bev, why?" he had pleaded then. "What did I do?"

"You didn't do anything," Bev had said, angry that he wouldn't just let her go and guilty that she had betrayed him. "I just don't love you anymore."

"It's him, isn't it?" Darren had accused her. "Jim Randall at the yard. You're after him."

"What if I am?" she had said cruelly. "It's none of your business."

"But I love you!" he said. "Doesn't that mean anything?"

"I'm sorry!" was her only reply. She had started to cry and had run away.

She was filled anew with guilt and remorse.

Within a few moments her breathing returned to normal, and she slowly continued to wend her way through town. But the joy of the day had disappeared.

Lorraine knew by Bev's mood that something had happened on her walk through town, and it didn't take much guessing to figure out what.

"You saw Darren, didn't you?" she said. The two were preparing vegetables for dinner.

"Yes," Bev said. "It was pretty bad. He was so distant and—" Bev put down her knife and walked to the window, her back to her sister. "He's still hurt by what I did."

"He was so in love with you," Lorraine said, wiping her hands and coming to stand by her sister. "Like everyone else in town, he assumed that you two would get married and settle here and raise your family and be happy ever after. He never anticipated that you would fall for someone else and leave him."

Bev stood rigid, quiet tears running down her cheeks. She wiped them away almost angrily. "You know what's so sad," she said. Lorraine shook her head. "I still love him."

Lorraine didn't seem surprised.

"I don't think I ever really stopped. Seeing him today was almost a physical blow. He was suddenly just standing there and it was like we were kids again and I could reach up and touch his face and he'd wink and kiss me—" She leaned heavily into Lorraine's shoulder. "But I don't think he loves me any more," she said with a heavy sigh. "He was so cold, so distant. Oh, what am I going to do?"

"You're going to get up tomorrow morning and go to your reunion and not worry about what the next day or the next after that brings," Lorraine said.

"I don't know if I can," Bev said. "We were Beaverbrook High's golden couple. I'm afraid I'm coming back rather tarnished."

"I think you'll be surprised about how many people don't care about all that," Lorraine said. "You need to do this."

Bev nodded and walked out of the room.

"And I need to make a phone call," Lorraine said quietly.

THE NEXT DAY was rainy and cold, matching Bev's mood perfectly. She showed little enthusiasm for the prospect of attending the reunion, but was nonetheless swept up into preparations by her sister and daughter.

"Wear the burgundy Indian cotton dress, Mom," Christy said. "It looks great on you."

"I think you should pull your hair back, show off your face," Lorraine said.

"I'll do your makeup," Christy offered.

"I don't really think it matters too much what I wear, you two," Bev said sourly.

"Nonsense," Lorraine said. "No one has seen you in twenty years. You need to make a sharp impression."

"All I'm going to be is an object of curiosity," Bev said bitterly.

"Then be a gorgeous object," Christy said.

Bev made a face as Lorraine and Christy giggled. She just wanted the day to be over.

Once over her initial nervousness, which started when she got out of her car at the high school and intensified as she approached the registration table, Bev found herself enjoying the reunion.

She had run into many old classmates and a few old teachers, and despite her certainty that she would be the center of uncomfortable scrutiny, she found that most were happy to see her. The reunion committee had set up displays for each of the twenty years' graduating classes, and Bev was soon immersed in reliving old memories in the '80–'81 room.

"We all look so young," said a short, plump woman Bev finally recognized as Tina, the yearbook committee president.

"Yes, don't we?" Bev said. "Young and with the whole world waiting for us."

"You were Darren McKenny's girlfriend, weren't you?" Tina said, scanning the photos on the wall.

Bev's heart skipped a beat, but she swallowed and said, "Yes, a long time ago."

"Shame you two broke up," Tina went on. Then she pointed, "Oo, here it is! I knew I'd find it."

Bev looked at the photo. It was taken on prom night, and she and Darren had been crowned King and Queen of the prom. The caption read, "Most likely to reign together forever." Two months later, that smiling, pretty girl had broken the heart of that smiling, handsome boy.

"Nice looking couple," said a male voice behind them.

Bev whirled around to face Darren.

He smiled as Tina squealed and said, "We were just talking about you!"

"Were you now," Darren said, not taking his eyes off Bev's startled face.

Tina looked from one to the other and smiled herself. "See you two around!"

They didn't notice her leave. They stood once again just gazing at each other, Bev trying to fathom what was different about Darren this time.

He turned his head and nodded at the prom photo. "We were a cute couple," he said.

And it hit Bev. His reserve was gone. He even smiled, and there before her was her lost love, the boy she'd left behind.

"A lot of years have gone by since then," she said.

"A lot of growing up, too," he said.

"Were you terribly unhappy these past twenty years?"

"Only sometimes."

"I'm sorry. So very, very sorry."

"I am, too."

Bev looked at him sharply. "Why are you sorry?"

"I'm sorry that I didn't fight harder to keep you."

"I didn't give you much of a chance, did I?"

"I could have tried, at least. And I'm sorry your life didn't turn out like you expected."

Bev gasped. "How did you—?" *Of course, Lorraine.* "I made the choice. I lived with the consequences. I have three great kids. I don't regret them."

"What now?"

"I—I think—" and she looked at him again, examining and reading messages in his eyes and wondering what it was she did want. And then she knew. "I think it's time to come home," she said.

He smiled and nodded. "Maybe it is, at that."

They stood in companionable silence a few moments longer, looking at the picture of the young and innocent couple. Each silently bade farewell to the ghosts of their old mistakes and felt no regret at letting them go.

"There's a dance later," Darren said. "I was wondering—"

"I'd love to," Bev said, her smile filled with warmth and the emotions that lay just beneath the surface. Perhaps he sensed what was there, or maybe Lorraine had told him, but his smile was full of promise.

"Great!" he said. "It'll be like old times."

Bev took one last look at the photo. "No, it'll be like new times." And she smiled at Darren.

They say that you can't go home again. Bev was beginning to think that maybe they were wrong.

Always the Bridesmaid

*J*enna watched Scott and Nancy take their vows and felt the bile of disappointment, quickly followed by shame, rise in her.

It was always this way for her at weddings, and there had been so many weddings these last couple of years, as the marriageable—the lucky—paired up and pledged their lives together. But not for Jenna this bliss of falling in love and planning her one perfect day. Not for her the giddy round of bridal showers and the envious glances of the still unwed. Because, you see, fat girls don't find true love.

Jenna frowned and tried to put her mind on the ceremony.

"And do you, Nancy, take Scott to be your lawfully wedded husband?"

"I do." Nancy's voice was a whisper.

Jenna felt the tears threatening and she swallowed hard, trying to dislodge the lump of self-pity that sat in her throat.

I will not cry, she said in her head, like a mantra. *I will not cry.* For these were not tears of joy at her best friend's happiness, but bitter tears, angry tears.

"Please stand up with me," Nancy had pleaded those many months ago. "You are my very best friend in the whole world. Please!"

"I'd look ridiculous, Nance," Jenna had said, rather cruelly in retrospect. "You are a tiny, perfect bride-to-be. I'd look like some ungainly behemoth beside you."

"That's not true!" Nancy had gotten angry as she almost always did at Jenna's self-deprecating remarks. "You *are* pretty." She glared at Jenna's derisive snort. "God, I hate how you talk about yourself."

"I only speak the truth."

"Bull! You need to stop feeling sorry for yourself and take a look at yourself. See what others see. See what I see."

"They see a five-foot-eleven, four-hundred-pound freak!"

"That's not what I see."

"Oh, Nance. If Cujo walked in here, all you'd see was a cute little puppy."

"Damn it, Jenna!" Nancy had stamped her foot for emphasis. "You are, and always have been, the best friend I have ever had. You are funny and smart. You have a generous heart and a wise and sensitive soul. Why do you have this horrible vision of yourself?"

"Gee, I don't know," Jenna said sourly. "Could be all the hundreds of times it's been pointed out to me."

"Just because stupid people say stupid things doesn't mean you have to believe them."

"Hey, they *all* can't be wrong."

So Jenna had not stood beside Nancy on this, her special day. Guilt joined self-pity and formed an acid knot in Jenna's belly.

Jenna did have a place of honor with Nancy's parents, whom Jenna thought of as her second set. And she had worked hard to look nice for the day, foregoing her usual baggy camouflage wear for a quite stylish, dressy palazzo-pants-and-tunic set in deep hunter green. The simple tunic was heavily beaded with irridescent beads around the neckline and down the front.

Jenna felt elegant, if not exactly pretty.

BUT A PAIR OF EYES across the church thought Jenna was very pretty indeed.

Barrington Lockhart had almost not come to the wedding. At

nearly 40, he had seen more than his share, and with his cynical view on the institution of marriage, he felt he could happily miss another disaster in the making. Barrington was the kind of confirmed bachelor who avoided marriage out of a certainty that all such unions were doomed to failure.

He'd never met a woman who set his pulse racing or who caused his resolve to waver. He had been accused by many of having impossibly high standards. He just figured there was something wrong with him. His last girlfriend had said it best: "The trouble with you, Barry, is that you have no heart." At the time, he applauded her insight.

But now he doubted the veracity of those words, because the organ in his chest was beating rather erratically. And the cause was a glorious red-haired goddess in green. He was filled with gratitude for Jim's insistence that he be at Scott and Nancy's wedding.

"Hey, my kid only gets married once, you know."

Barry chose not to argue with Jim's rosy view on life.

Now his eyes took in the beauty's shoulder-length, rich auburn hair, her cute little nose and determined chin. He longed to see her smile and hear her voice. He found himself wishing for the ceremony to be done, not only so he could finally stretch his six-foot-four frame now so uncomfortably squashed in the pew, but so he could sooner arrange an introduction to the shapely beauty who had so surprisingly piqued his interest.

"I NOW PRONOUNCE YOU man and wife," intoned the minister. "You may kiss your bride."

The congregation laughed and applauded the couple's passionate embrace. The organist launched into the joyful triumphal march and the newlyweds, so confident and sure in their love for one another, strode down the aisle together.

Jenna's eyes, wistful tears threatening, followed their exit.

"Well, that's the last of the chicks from the nest," Jim said, giving his wife, Marie, a peck on the cheek.

"Yes, I suppose," Marie said, sniffing back her own tears. "But wait," she said, turning to Jenna. "We still have our Jenna to marry off, don't we?"

Jenna felt her face redden.

"No worries, Mrs. Landry," Jenna said, trying to keep her tone light and nonchalant. "I'm in no rush."

"Well, I'm sure, now that Nancy's a married lady," Marie said, patting Jenna's arm, "she'll be anxious to find you a special someone."

God, I hope not, Jenna thought. But she just smiled noncommittally.

Outside, bride and groom greeted their guests and basked in the love and support of family and friends.

BARRY HAD MOMENTARILY lost sight of the gorgeous redhead in the crush to get out of the church. His stomach clenched, fearful that she may have gone. But then, like a glorious burst of autumn color, she was there, not six feet from where he stood.

She was tall, he saw, and held herself with quiet grace. She was leaning over to better hear an elderly woman speaking to her. She still wore the serious expression on her face that she had worn in the church, but then something the old woman said caused her to laugh. Barry was sure he had never heard a more melodic sound. No music had ever moved him as much as the warm, rich, full tone of that burst of laughter. He felt uplifted, reborn, and more certain than ever of his need to meet this glorious creature.

He found that the receiving line had moved forward and he was shaking hands with Jim and Marie.

"Say, Barry," Jim said, pumping Barry's hand with enthusiasm, "I'm so glad you decided to come. Great day, isn't it?"

Jim's unfailing joviality was one of the things Barry admired about his business associate. He marveled that Jim always found the silver lining in any situation.

"Congratulations, Jim," Barry said, and then nodded toward Marie. "Congratulations. It was a nice ceremony." He never knew quite what to say in these forced social moments.

"Wasn't it?" Marie sighed, clasping her hands together.

"Um—do you suppose—" Barry reddened, suddenly embarrassed to be asking the next question. Then he caught sight once again of the red-haired vision, now talking to the bride and groom. "Who is that talking to your daughter?"

Jim and Marie both looked.

"That's our Jenna," Marie said, and smiled. "She's Nancy's best friend. They practically grew up together. In fact, Jim and I think of Jenna as another daughter. Come on, I'll introduce you."

Barry was propelled along by the diminutive Marie and felt his breath squeezing out of his body as they neared the object of his growing desire. Warm brown eyes rose to greet them as Jenna stood to her full height. Was it wariness Barry detected in them?

"You know my daughter," Jim said, kissing Nancy on her cheek.

"Hi, Mr. Lockhart," Nancy said sweetly. "Thank you for coming."

"Much happiness to you both," he said, casting surreptitious glances at the tense, quiet woman beside her.

"This is Scott—my husband," the bride said, blushing prettily.

The two men shook hands and Barry's pulse picked up tempo as he turned to be introduced to Nancy's gorgeous friend.

JENNA LOOKED UP into a pair of serious blue eyes and for a moment had the oddest sensation of pitching forward, as if about to fall from a great height. She was glad of Nancy's arm, now linked through hers, for she was certain she would teeter over without the support.

"And this is my best friend in the whole world, Jenna McCauley," Nancy said. "Jenna, this is Mr. Lockhart. He and dad work in the same department at the plant."

A large, warm hand took Jenna's weakly proffered one. She stared at the joining of her skin to his and was sharply conscious of the wave of sensation coursing up her arm. She was intensely aware of his proximity, and yet all else around her had faded far off to the distance. She jumped slightly when he spoke, his voice sharply clear in her ear.

"A pleasure to meet you, Jenna."

She exhaled deeply. She was aware of her eyes slowly closing and opening as if he had kissed her. Heat flooded through her at daring to think this thought.

"Please, call me Barry."

"Barry," she said, her voice barely above a choked whisper. Their eyes met and held, and each of them felt their worlds shift and collide. They surfaced moments later, immeasurably changed.

"—so we'll see you at the reception, I hope." Marie's voice filtered into the rarefied air surrounding Jenna and Barry.

Jenna was the first to break free of the spell. "W-what?" She felt drunk and fuzzy.

"I was just asking Barry if he was going to the reception," Marie said. She looked from one to the other, a strange expression on her face.

"Excuse me," Jenna said, and made a panicked escape.

SHE FOUND REFUGE in her car. Her breath was labored and she had a painful stitch in her side. She couldn't seem to get her thoughts in any logical order. Random impressions kept flitting through her mind. A warm smile, deep soulful eyes, broad shoulders, big hands, long legs, wavy hair, rumbling voice, spicy cologne.

"Damn it!" she said, hitting her hand on the steering wheel. She had run away like some scared little chicken from the big bad wolf. What an ass she was. Right this second Barry was likely thanking his lucky stars that Marie had spoken to them when she had. What an idiot she must have seemed, standing there like some—love struck ninny! Tears welled in her eyes. She sniffed them away.

She pushed the key into the ignition and started the car. Hardly aware of her intentions, she jammed it into gear and, with an embarrassing squeal of tires, pulled out of the parking lot. Once on the road, the sense of panic dissipated a bit. She rolled down the window and let the rushing air cool her skin. Common sense finally made her slow down to within the speed limit, and she headed the car out of town.

I hurt my dearest friend in the world by not standing up with her today, all because of my pitiful low self-esteem. She was right. I never try and look at myself to see what it is others see. If I did, would it be so bad?

A vision of a pair of intent eyes and a warm smile filled her mind. What had Barry seen when he looked at her like that?

She found she really wanted to know. She jammed on the brakes and pulled a U-turn, suddenly sure of where she needed to go.

BARRY HAD WATCHED Jenna's flight and felt at that moment as if he was in the grip of some powerful dream. Now he sat in the coffee shop, his hands wrapped around a mug. Every few moments he took a disinterested sip of the hot brew. His mind was a turmoil of questions.

What had made Jenna run away? Should he have said something to her? But then his mind couldn't have formed a coherent sentence if he'd tried. What a jackass he'd been. Here was this gorgeous woman and all he'd had to do was say, "May I escort you to the reception?" Simple. Was that it? Was she angry he hadn't asked? Was that why she'd left so abruptly?

Barry signaled the waitress for a refill and then was struck by the humor of his situation. He chuckled.

"Somethin' funny, mister?" the tired-looking waitress said.

Barry looked at her and grinned. He dug his wallet out of his pocket and slapped a far-too-large bill on the counter.

"Keep the change, sweetheart."

"You win the lottery or somethin'?" The waitress picked up the money and looked at Barry as if he'd sprouted wings.

"Or something," he said, and strode out of the coffee shop.

JENNA FELT THE MUSIC and laughter wash over her as she entered the banquet hall where the wedding reception was in full swing. A squeal of delight announced that the bride had seen her, and Jenna laughed when her friend grabbed her in a clumsy hug.

"Oh, I'm so glad you're here," Nancy said.

"Wouldn't miss this for the world," Jenna said. "Now, do you think you could let me breathe?"

Nancy released her and giggled. "Sorry. Too much champagne, I guess."

Jenna looked at Nancy's flushed cheeks and shining eyes. She was the picture of happy.

"Look, I want to say something to you before you get pulled away," Jenna said.

"Better hurry. I see my husband coming this way."

"I just wanted to tell you how sorry I am that I let you down."

"Let me down?" Nancy looked genuinely puzzled. "What do you mean?"

"I'm sorry I didn't stand up with you today."

Nancy put her hand on Jenna's arm. "Look, don't worry about it. I understand. You didn't feel comfortable and—"

"But I should have done it anyway! I was scared people would laugh at me."

"No one would—"

"You don't have to say it." Jenna took a deep breath. "I just realized that you were right. I don't try to see the me that others see. I let fear run my life, and because of that I miss out on so much wonderful stuff. So, I've made a decision."

"What decision is that?" Nancy looked up solemnly at her friend's impassioned face.

"I've decided that from now on, I'm going to swallow my fears and do whatever I wish to do, without worrying about what other people will think."

Nancy grinned and hugged Jenna again. "Good for you!"

"May I steal my new bride for a dance?"

The two girls moved apart, and Scott put his arm around Nancy and bent to kiss her softly.

Jenna smiled. "Absolutely," she said. "Just make sure to save a dance for me later. I have a few words of advice for you since I've known Nance all my life."

"Count on it!" he said with a grin as he steered the protesting Nancy to the dance floor.

"They make a lovely couple," said a deep voice that reverberated through Jenna's body, leaving her tingling all over. She turned

46

and found herself intoxicatingly close to Barry Lockhart.

"Yes," she said, her voice breathy and deep. "They're well matched."

"That's important, " he said, his eyes roving over her face as if to imprint it in his memory, "to find that special someone that matches you."

"A soul mate."

"Yes, a soul mate." The two stood silent for a moment, speaking but not speaking. Each smiled and knew the other understood.

"I was afraid you weren't coming," Barry said, and he ran his hand from her shoulder to her hand and then captured her fingers in his.

Jenna's eyes followed his gesture, and she was sure her heart stopped for a beat or two. She looked deep into his blue eyes and saw questions there. "I almost didn't," she admitted.

"What changed your mind?" he asked.

"You."

"Me?" Barry looked genuinely surprised.

Jenna blushed. "I guess you could say I was tired of lost chances."

Barry smiled. "I confess, I overheard what you said to Nancy."

"Oh." Jenna's shoulders sagged. She waited for the inevitable kind words.

"I'm relieved."

Jenna's head snapped up and she looked at Barry. He was smiling. "What?"

"I'm relieved. Relieved that it wasn't me that scared you off."

Jenna laughed. "I was afraid that I'd made a fool of myself again, gaping at you like some silly schoolgirl."

"I was afraid you were angry at me for not asking to escort you to the reception."

They both laughed.

"What a pair we are," Jenna said, and she felt compelled to run her fingers down his cheek. She blushed and tried to turn away as she realized what she had done. Warm fingers touched her chin and pulled her gently back.

Before Jenna could comprehend what was happening, strong lips pressed against hers. Two strong arms pulled her close and her own arms wound around his neck. As quickly as it had begun, it was over, but Jenna and Barry both were inexplicably changed at the end of it.

Their foreheads touched and both were grateful for the support of the other as legs trembled weakly.

"We are a pair," Barry said, his voice husky with emotion. "I think I knew that when I first saw you across the church."

"I feel it, too," Jenna said. "I felt it when I first looked into your eyes."

"I've never been very good at this relationship thing," Barry said.

"Neither have I, but maybe together we can get it right?"

Barry pulled back and looked at Jenna's glowing face. God, but she was beautiful! "I'd like to try, Jenna."

"Me, too."

And they smiled.

"I had a feeling about you two!"

They jumped apart and found Marie beaming up at the two of them. "Now, the party is in there, and as much as the two of you I'm sure would like to continue to smooch out here in the foyer—"

Jenna blushed and Barry laughed.

"—I think it's high time you get in there and join the celebration. Nancy's about to throw the bouquet!" With a wink in Jenna's direction, she was gone.

"Well, shall we?" Barry swept an arm across his chest and bowed.

Jenna laughed and curtsied in return. "I would be delighted." She took his arm and with pride and new hope in their hearts, the couple joined the festivities.

Blue Collar Knight

"I am so tired." Tess took one hand off the wheel and shook it. "I think my hands are losing their feeling."

"We have been on the road for—" Marcie looked at her watch. "—four hours. We're overdue for a break."

"I really wanted to make it home before dark," Tess said, rolling her head from side to side, "but I don't think I can do it, not after the week we've just had."

Marcie grinned. "It was fun, wasn't it?"

"Totally!" Tess grinned back.

"And don't give me that 'home before dark' crap," Marcie said. "You can't wait to get home to your husband and jump him."

"It's been a week!" Tess said. "I am in serious sex withdrawal!"

"I don't want to know," Marcie said, holding up her hand.

"You brought it up," Tess said. "Speaking of which—"

"Tess!"

Tess just laughed. "Hey, there's a Country Oven sign. What does it say?"

"It says there's one 37 miles ahead."

"Hallelujah. Food, washroom, and some shopping. What more could a girl want?"

"A chocolate sundae!"

"Amen to that," Tess said, and pressed her foot down on the pedal. "Just keep your eyes open for any cops."

The Country Oven was a familiar stop for the two friends. They had met just after college at their first Living Large national convention and had been traveling buddies ever since. The restaurant chain was like an old friend that welcomed them wherever they happened to go.

"I am starving." Marcie perused the menu carefully.

"Yeah, me too," Tess said.

The waitress sidled up to their table with a pitcher of water and filled their glasses.

"So what can I get you ladies today?" she asked in that universal perky waitress voice.

"Whatever is good," Tess said with a friendly smile.

"Hungry, are we?"

"You said it!"

Marcie's brow was furrowed in her concentration over the menu.

"It all looks good," she said with a sigh.

"Well, make up your mind," Tess said. "I have a hubby to get home to!"

The girls placed their orders and just allowed themselves to relax. Marcie took out her diary and made a notation.

"You aren't writing about us stopping for dinner, are you?" Tess shook her head. "If you recorded my trip to the restroom, I'll shoot you!"

"Oh, stop teasing me." Marcie blushed. "It's perfectly natural to want a record of our trip. I love to read about it later and relive the highlights."

"Highlights, yes," Tess said, "but every little mundane moment? Really, Marcie, we just *have* to get you a life!"

The waitress arrived with their dinners.

"There you are, ladies. Enjoy."

The two women suspended conversation to concentrate on

the fragrant dishes before them. Once initial hunger was appeased, Marcie picked up the thread of their discussion.

"I do have a life, you know!"

"Oh? Let's see—" Tess held up a hand and started ticking off a list. "You work at an elementary school. Lots of thrills there. You sing in the church choir. You knit like a whiz. You're a pretty good cook—"

"Pretty good!"

Tess laughed. "Face it, girlfriend. You have a nice life, but it's hardly thrilling." Something behind Marcie caught Tess's eye and she frowned. But she picked up her fork and resumed eating. The waitress arrived at their table once more.

"How is everything?"

"Good," Marcie said. Tess looked at the waitress intently, but said nothing.

"Will you be ordering dessert?"

Tess looked at Marcie and raised an inquisitive brow. Marcie nodded and they placed their orders.

"My mouth is all set for that chocolate sundae," Marcie said to Tess. "And if that makes me a less-than-thrilling person, well, I like it that way." Marcie sat up primly and brushed imaginary crumbs off her blouse. She glanced up, waiting for Tess's next teasing jibe, and caught a look of anger crossing her friend's face. For a moment she thought it was directed at her, then she realized Tess was look-ing at a point over her shoulder.

"What?"

Tess shook her head and didn't answer. Once more, the perky waitress breezed up to their table. She set down their desserts and picked up their empty plates.

"Coffee?" she said. The two ordered and she was gone again. Marcie saw Tess following the waitress's movements intently, a frown turning into a scowl on her face.

"Did you see that?" Tess said, her eyes flashing sparks of fury.

"What?" Marcie said through a mouthful of chocolate fudge sundae.

"You know, that really ticks me off!" Tess said, slamming her fork on the table, her cheesecake forgotten.

"What?"

"Our waitress!" Tess was glaring over Marcie's shoulder.

"What about our waitress?" Marcie started to turn to look.

"Don't look!" Tess barked. "Don't give them the satisfaction." Her plump arms were crossed and indignation was written all over her.

"Don't give who the satisfaction?" Marcie always got a little nervous when Tess got like this. And Tess got like this every time they came home from the Living Large national convention.

Marcie and Tess were both what was euphemistically called "plus sized." In truth, both women were well over the three-hundred-pound mark, distributed over almost six-foot frames. Two women that tall and that size got noticed, and not always in a positive way.

"That snippy waitress of ours just now dragged a fourth person to the kitchen door and pointed us out."

"A fourth person?"

"I've been watching," Tess said in a low voice. "Since she took our order, she has marched one person after another to the door, pointed at us and had a laugh or two."

"Are you sure that's what she's been doing?"

Tess looked at Marcie as if she were simple.

"Oh, I'm sure, all right," she said. "And I'll be damned if I'm going to sit here and let her get away with it." Tess's voice was rising in volume. Marcie looked around the now crowded restaurant. Several patrons near their table were looking. Marcie's face felt hot with embarrassment.

"Look, Tess," she said softly. "I know you're all fired up after a week at the convention, but do you think we should make a big deal?'

Tess raised her eyebrows in surprise at Marcie's question.

"This is exactly when we should make a big deal. This is what Living Large is all about, ridding society of this insidious size prejudice. This kind of behavior is no different than those guys that wear "No Fat Chick" T-shirts or kids that make farm animal noises when we walk by. If we sit here and let that cheesy little blonde get away with this, then we are in effect telling everyone that it's all right to make fun of fat people. Well, it's not!"

By this point Tess's voice was ringing out clearly in her anger, and more of the dining room had tuned in to the unfolding drama. The odd self-conscious snicker could be heard, but also a small pattering of applause. Marcie tried to sink down into her seat. The remainder of her chocolate sundae sat before her, but she had lost her appetite. All she wanted to do was flee. But she knew she was trapped.

Their waitress appeared at the table. Marcie couldn't help but wonder if she detected a faint smirk on the girl's face.

"Can I get you ladies anything else?" she said in her chipper voice, a wide grin on her face.

"Yes, you can get the manager," Tess snapped. The waitress' grin vanished.

"Excuse me?"

Tess stood up and glared down at the now nervous woman.

"I said, get the manager—now!"

The hostess came scurrying over to their table. Marcie sank deeper into her seat.

"Excuse me, ma'am. Is there a problem here?"

"Yes there is!" Tess said clearly. "Your waitress was very rude to my friend and me—"

"I wasn't," sputtered the red-faced girl. Her eyes were wide, caught as she was in the glare of Tess's formidable anger.

"I'd like to speak to the manager!" Tess stood her ground, uncompromising and firm.

The hostess quickly exited and returned with a tall, lanky older gentleman. He glanced sternly at the now-mute waitress and turned to Tess.

"I understand that there is a problem." He spoke softly, an obvious attempt to smooth Tess's ruffled feathers and keep the situation under control. "We here at the Country Oven want our patrons to have a pleasant dining experience. How can I help?"

Tess was not to be mollified. She stood tall and straight and was just about able to look the manager directly in the eye. She spoke in equally reasonable tones.

"My friend and I have been traveling all day. We're returning from a size acceptance convention in Boston. All we wanted was a quiet dinner and a chance to rest. We have always found in the past that the Country Oven was a pleasant place to stop. But it seems that we have become the entertainment for the entire kitchen staff."

"We weren't laughing at you," the waitress blurted. She turned to look at her boss. "Really, we weren't! One of the guys told a joke about a white whale. That's what we were laughing at."

An uncomfortable pause followed her words and she flushed scarlet. Tess continued.

"I watched as she," she pointed at the now-squirming waitress, "marched person after person from the kitchen to the door. They looked very clearly at us and then burst into laughter. One time, maybe, is coincidence, but several times is deliberate rudeness."

Marcie had to admire how Tess stood proudly and didn't flinch from speaking her mind. She felt a little ashamed that she had allowed herself to slip into wallflower mode and let Tess stand alone. She wondered if she had learned anything from the Living Large seminars she'd attended. She pulled herself up straight in her chair and turned to glare at the offensive waitress.

"Let me apologize on behalf of the Country Oven. And please allow us to pay for your dinners. Rest assured, this matter will be dealt with." At that, he gestured for the waitress to follow him and they disappeared into the kitchen. Tess sat down and breathed a deep sigh.

"Wow," Marcie said, and grinned at her friend. "You were great!"

Tess grinned back. "I was, wasn't I? I don't know what came over me, but I just felt angry and this little voice said, 'go for it.' Once I got started, I couldn't stop."

"You were amazing," Marcie said. "I'm sorry I just sat here like—"

"Don't be silly!" Tess said, smiling at Marcie. "It was my battle.

I picked it. You can take on the next one, deal?"

"Deal," Marcie said with a grin. "It's lucky, though, that most people aren't like her, isn't it?"

Tess shook her head, a bemused smile on her face. "You know, you really are the last of the innocents," she said.

"What do you mean?" Marcie didn't know whether to be insulted or flattered.

"You always see the best in people, even if it isn't there."

"Oh come on, Tess. Everyone has something good about him or her. I'd rather look for that than to always be looking at negatives."

"See, that's what I mean. And don't get me wrong, I do admire your ability to see good in others. You have a generous and accepting nature."

Marcie blushed. "Thanks, Tess."

"But I do worry that it leaves you vulnerable. I hate seeing you get your heart broken time and again. People take advantage of you."

"Oh, a little hurt makes the joy all the more wonderful."

"You're hopeless," Tess said with laughter. "Well, try and toughen up a bit, okay?"

"Yes, boss, I'll try." Marcie gave a mock salute. "Wonder what Dave will say about your little protest."

"My dear hubby will shake his head and say something like, 'I'm not surprised.'" Both girls giggled. Dave adored his wife and often expressed how lucky he was to have married her.

"It's too bad Dave couldn't come to the convention this year," Marcie said.

"It's a building boom right now, poor baby," Tess said, "and he's the boss, so he couldn't get away." A wistful look came into her eyes. "I miss the big lug, though."

"You're so lucky," Marcie said. "I want to find what you two have. I just want to find a nice guy who thinks I'm beautiful, all of me. Is that asking too much?"

Tess smiled at Marcie's earnest plea. She had been down this road before with her friend. In fact, before Dave, she had been down that road many times herself.

"You had Paul," Tess said. Marcie nodded. "You two dated for almost a year. He was a nice guy, and he thought you were beautiful."

"Yes, but there wasn't any spark, you know?"

"You mean, he didn't melt your butter," Tess said. Marcie laughed and blushed.

"Well, yeah. I mean, you and Dave are so obviously in love," she said wistfully. "You just fit so well together."

"I'll say," Tess said, wiggling her eyebrows and giving Marcie a suggestive wink.

"Ew! Tess!" Marcie playfully punched her friend on the arm.

"What about that guy, Walter, who followed you around all week at the convention?" Tess said, ducking from the punch.

Marcie blushed. "He did not."

"He did too," Tess insisted. "Every time we turned around we were tripping over him. I was thinking seriously of demanding that he install some kind of warning system before someone got hurt!" The two women giggled.

"He was okay, I guess," Marcie said. "But I didn't feel that way about him. I don't want to just settle for someone. I want the real deal, like you and Dave—my own knight in shining armor to rescue me."

Tess patted her friend's hand.

"You'll find him, I'm sure of it. You're a beautiful woman with a huge heart. When you least expect it, you'll find him. Or he'll find you."

"From your lips to God's ear," Marcie said with a sigh. "Now let's get out of here and get you home to your husband."

"Amen to that, girlfriend! And this ought to make one hell of an entry into that diary of yours!"

THE DRIVE WENT SMOOTHLY for the next hour. The two women cranked up the radio on a golden oldies station and sang at the top of their lungs, bursting into gales of laughter, feeling giddy just to be alive. They were about an hour from home when the first sign of trouble appeared. A light drizzle started, and quickly turned into a steady rain. The *thwap, thwap* of the wipers provided a backbeat to Marcie's soft humming. Tess had turned off the radio to concentrate on the dark stretch of highway now slick with rain.

"I'll be glad to get off the highway. I'm really too tired to cope with this for long."

"Want me to take over?" Marcie asked.

"I'm *really* too tired to cope with your driving," Tess teased.

"Excuse me!" Marcie said with mock indignation, and punched Tess in the arm.

"Ow!" Tess said. Suddenly the car gave a lurch and there was a distinct grinding sound.

"Oh damn!" Tess said, holding tight to the wheel and easing the car over to the shoulder. The car started to shudder and an unpleasant smell wafted into the vehicle.

"What is it?" Marcie squeaked, her hands braced against the dash.

"Looks like the chariot is about to quit on us." Tess gently applied the brakes and the car came to a stop. Smoke immediately drifted out from under the hood.

"God damn it all to hell anyway!" Tess yanked her door open and climbed out into the rain. She quickly had the hood open.

"Are we on fire?" Marcie said through her open window. "Should I get out?"

"No, it's okay, no fire. But we aren't going anywhere fast. Well, damn!"

Tess got back in the car. She slammed her palm against the steering wheel and started yelling at the now-crippled vehicle.

"You couldn't wait and do this in town? You had to do this in the middle of the night in the middle of nowhere when we were so close to home? What did I ever do to you?"

"Well, what shall we do?" Marcie asked, worry etched on her face. She was not overly fond of the dark, and didn't like the idea of being stranded on the highway. Traffic whizzed by, not even slowing to gawk at the smoking car.

"I don't know—Wait!" Tess grabbed her satchel and started

digging through. "Dave got me a cell phone for Christmas, for emergencies. I haven't used it for ages, so I never think about it. Keep your fingers crossed that it's kept its charge. Ah, here it is. Now, if he'd just given me a Triple A membership."

"I've got an auto club card," Marcie volunteered. She started rooting through her own handbag for her wallet. She chimed a "Ta-da!" and waved her card at Tess.

"Good girl!" Tess said. "See? What a team." She hit the power button on the phone. "Great! We have power." Using Marcie's card, Tess called the auto club and arranged a tow. Then she called her husband.

"Hi Honey—want to get on your white steed and come and rescue a couple of damsels in distress?…Yep, Marcie had a card and by the way, we need to talk about…It's on its way…An hour! How come?… Oh. See you then. I love you." She chuckled as she signed off. "I got him out of the shower. He has to rinse off the soap and get dressed.

"Whoa! Too much information," Marcie said, holding her hands up as if in surrender. "I don't need to be visualizing your hubby naked."

"You should be so lucky," Tess said with a laugh. "Anyway, then he's coming for us. So we might as well get comfy and relax."

Traffic whooshed by the car and the girls sat silently for a moment or two, Tess thinking how wonderful it would be to see Dave, Marcie thankful that she wasn't alone.

"You have any gum?" they both said at the same time. They collapsed in laughter.

FORTY-FIVE MINUTES had passed when they saw welcome flashing lights approaching from the rear. The rain had stopped for now, and the tow truck was finally there. They watched as the driver dismounted and approached the car. At his friendly tap, Tess turned on the interior lights and wound down the window.

Marcie gasped as two deeply intense eyes framed by thick lashes peered in the window. The slender, attractive man sized up the two women and grinned. *Hmm, cocky,* Marcie thought.

"So you ladies called for a tow?"

"We sure did," Tess quipped. "Can you take a look under the hood and tell me if there's any hope or if you should just hook her up now and drag her away?"

He flashed another great smile and winked at a now-blushing Marcie. Was it her imagination or was he flirting with her? Tess looked at her and raised her eyebrows. Apparently Tess thought so, too.

Marcie frowned. *Just like a man, to think he's God's gift to womankind.*

"Glad to, ma'am. Name's Mike."

"Tess, and this is my friend, Marcie."

"Always glad to help pretty ladies."

"Ooo, I like that—" Tess looked at Mike a little more closely. "Say, aren't you the new guy at Pete's garage?"

"Yeah. You know Pete?"

"Sure do. Not only does he fix our cars, but he beats my husband at poker the third Friday of every month."

Mike laughed. "Yeah, he's told me some stories about those games."

Tess got out and went to the front of the car with Mike. Marcie sat glued to her seat. She was seething.

"Pretty ladies" indeed. Just like a too-good-looking blue-collar jerk to make fun of two fat chicks. He'll probably get his kicks telling all his blue-jeaned, plaid-shirted good ol' buddies about the two heifers he rescued.

She heard Tess laugh and wondered why her normally astute friend couldn't see right through him.

She did have to admit he'd been nothing but polite and affable. Why was she having this knee-jerk negative reaction? She decided it was because he was just too good looking. And guys like him were rarely receptive to girls like her.

The open hood provided her with a framed view of Mike's trim waist and narrow hips. Her eyes were drawn to the center of this view and she gasped, realizing that she was staring at a stranger's crotch. The interior of the car felt suddenly very warm and claustrophobic.

Marcie pushed open her door and hopped out, nearly tipping over into the ditch. She was grateful that Mike couldn't read her mind and see the vivid licentious thoughts he had inspired there. Not that he'd care anyway. It would just add more spice to his tale for the boys. Tess continued to chatter away

"—so I called my husband. He should be here any time now."

"Is your friend married?"

"Marcie? Why no, she's not. You?" Marcie held her breath, embarrassed that they were talking about her. She could just shoot Tess for that.

"Nah, I'm free as a bird. I'm looking, though." His chuckle was deep and rumbly, and put goose bumps on Marcie's arms.

"Oh?"

"Yeah. It's hard to meet people though, you know?"

Marcie slid herself forward so she could see them clearly illuminated in the headlights.

"I don't like bars or clubs. For one thing, I don't drink—well, maybe a beer now and then. But I don't like all the phoniness in those places. The girls all seem to be so plastic. I want a real woman in my life."

"What kind of woman is that?" Tess pressed on. Marcie moved closer, intrigued to hear his answer.

Mike stood and looked thoughtfully at Tess. "Well, a real woman is soft and warm. She has a good heart and quick mind and would be loyal and true to the man in her life. With a real woman, I'd know she had good values and wasn't always grasping for material things. A real woman would appreciate that I'm a good-hearted, hard-working guy, if not the best-looking or the richest."

"So you basically want a woman who will worship at your feet and take care of you," Marcie found herself interjecting in accusatory tones. She was as surprised by her attack as Tess's expression showed she was. But some impulse inside made her plow forward. "Well?"

"That's not what I said," Mike replied, a cool edge to his words.

Marcie's stomach tightened and she moved around to stand by Tess. *Safety in numbers,* she thought.

Tess got a firm grip on Marcie's arm. "You'll have to excuse Marcie here," she said, trying to break the tension with some levity. "Lack of sleep has made her punchy."

Marcie wisely held her tongue.

"What I *was* saying," Mike continued, some of his flirtatious good humor gone, "is that I'd make it my prime objective to make a woman like that happy." He directed his comments to Tess. Marcie felt the snub and was ashamed at having earned it.

"And you haven't found someone like that yet?"

"Aw, I thought I had a couple of times, but it didn't work out. You see, well—never mind." Mike flushed and suddenly bent over the engine, intent on looking busy.

"Probably got tired of being an object—*ow!*" Marcie rubbed her arm where Tess had pinched her.

"Finish what you were saying," Tess said gently.

Marcie leaned against the front fender of the car, feigning indifference. Mike didn't seem to notice her there, so she took the opportunity to take in his broad shoulders, strong arms and long legs. He really was very nice to look at. Too bad he was just like the rest. He stood up and wiped his hand on a rag he pulled from his back jeans pocket.

"Well, I like a certain—type of girl, and when I was younger it wasn't a popular choice among my friends. And I was wimpy enough to bow to the pressure and date girls who really weren't my type. Thankfully I got older and I got wiser and the guys' wisecracks didn't bother me so much. I decided then that if I was going to be happy, I had to date the type of women I was attracted to and not compromise anymore."

Tess nodded as if she understood and smiled her support. Marcie was confused. He wasn't talking like she thought he should.

"Look, I meant it earlier, at the window, when I said you were pretty ladies." He flushed again but looked hard at Tess, daring her, Marcie supposed, to argue with him. She blanched. It suddenly occurred to her that she might have misjudged him.

"You're what we call at Living Large 'a big girl's dream,'" Tess said.

"Living Large?"

"It's a size acceptance group we belong to, right, Marcie?" Tess gestured to Marcie, who stepped around Mike to face him.

Marcie blushed. "Um, yes."

"And we've just come from the convention. It's a remarkable experience, and it might explain my friend's rather pre-emptive attack on your character."

"Oh?" He cast a speculative look in Marcie's direction.

"Look, I'm sorry," she blurted. "We had an episode at the restaurant and I sat there like a lump and when I thought you might be making fun of us I just kind of blew a fuse. I'm normally not—" She was delivering this at top speed. Pausing to breathe, she saw Mike grin and heard Tess's chuckle. If possible, her face got redder and she snapped her mouth shut.

"Ah, the real Marcie revealed at last!"

"Okay, you guys," Marcie said with a smile. "Are you enjoying this laugh at my expense?'

"Absolutely!" Tess and Mike said in unison.

"So," Mike said, favoring Marcie with a smile that she returned in full measure. "So you two were heading home."

"Yes," she said shyly. She smiled and was pleased to see Mike's smile widen in response. "We're just coming home from the national convention." She felt Tess step back slightly, cleverly putting Marcie into the forefront to carry on the conversation. "We've both been members for about eight years now, basically since shortly after college. It's a wonderful source of support and strength. It's for Lovely Large Women and their admirers. Tess met her husband there five years ago."

"Really." Mike looked fascinated. He leaned against the car and bent slightly toward Marcie. "So they have conventions. And it's just ladies like you and Tess and guys like me who—like them?"

"Basically," Marcie said, beginning to relax. She was surprised to find that Mike was easy to talk to.

"And how does somebody find out about this Living Large organization?" He smiled invitingly at Marcie, and she felt that smile to the tips of her toes. Their eyes locked. His said, *I like what I see.* Hers said, *I feel the same way.*

"I'd be happy—"

The blare of a horn announced Dave's arrival.

"There's my sweet hubby now," Tess said, waving frantically at the approaching SUV. Dave pulled up in front of the crippled car and hopped out. In three strides he reached Tess and, ignoring the other two, swept Tess into a bear hug.

Marcie grinned at the exuberance of his embrace. He was a gentle giant of a man, and loved his wife to distraction.

"One blue collar knight to the rescue," he said, giving Tess a loud, smacking kiss.

"Oooo, I missed you, you big lug," Tess cried and, wrapping her arms around his neck, kissed him back with gusto.

Mike chuckled at the demonstration.

"Are they always like this?"

"Sometimes they're even worse," Marcie said, shaking her head and laughing. She let out a big sigh. "They're so lucky."

"Lucky?" Mike caught the wistful look on Marcie's face.

"To have found each other. They're so perfect for each other. I wish—" She stopped and glanced at Mike and then glanced away. She hoped the darkness hid the flush on her cheeks.

"They say that there's someone for everyone in the world," Mike mused.

"So I've heard," Marcie said, her eyes watching Tess and Dave laugh and tease. "The trick is figuring out who that someone is."

"It's not so hard," Mike said softly. Somehow he was suddenly closer to her. Marcie was aware of him with every nerve in her body. "You just have to make sure you're looking when the some-one appears."

Marcie tilted her head and found herself falling into Mike's dreamy eyes.

"Oh?" she said breathily.

"So, are you looking, Marcie?" Mike's face tilted toward Marcie's. Her heart pounded. Blood roared in her ears and then all breath left her body as his warm, soft lips pressed lightly to hers.

Her mind screamed *NO* as he stood back. It was over too soon.

She opened her eyes and looked shyly at Mike. He grinned, and his eyes twinkled with mischief and delight. She knew then that she was smitten.

"Hey, Marcie!" a voice intruded. It irritated Marcie. *Who would be trying—? Oh no!* Marcie shook her head in a vain attempt to clear her mind. Mike was acting like a narcotic on her system.

"Um—yeah?" She turned to Tess and saw the wide grin on her friend's face. Her own face flushed scarlet, and she was sure she glowed in the dark.

"Dave and I were wondering if you could do us a favor."

"What?"

"Well, we're a little anxious to get going—" Tess giggled as Dave fondled her backside playfully. "We were wondering if you mind going with the car and making sure it gets to the garage safely. And Mike?"

"Yeah?"

"Could you maybe give Marcie a lift home after you've dropped off the car?"

Mike grinned in approval at the plan.

"I'd be happy to!" He looked at Marcie. "Is that okay with you?"

Marcie felt swept along on some tidal rush, but she was giddy with the excitement of it. She nodded.

Mike's grin widened. "Looks like a deal."

Marcie got the keys from Tess, and Mike went to get the truck. The two women hugged and Tess whispered, "It looks like we both got rescued tonight."

"Thanks, Tess," Marcie whispered back, "especially for bailing me out after goodness knows what came over me."

Tess chuckled. "I know we had a deal that you'd fight the next battle. But do you think next time you could be sure there actually is a battle?"

"Deal," Marcie said.

"It looks like maybe you just got that life we were talking about." Tess grinned at her friend.

Marcie glanced over to Mike and then grinned back. "I think you could be right."

She watched Tess and Dave drive off and for a brief moment questioned the wisdom of staying alone on the highway at night with a relative stranger. She watched as Mike maneuvered the truck into place and set about hitching the car to the back. He worked quickly and expertly, and then turned to her and smiled. And all her doubts fled. She was safe.

"Well, that's that. Shall we, milady? Your steed awaits." He lifted his cap and swept it theatrically through the air as he bowed deeply.

Marcie gasped. "How did you know?" But then she knew the answer. Every self-respecting knight, even the blue-collar variety, recognizes a damsel in distress when he sees one.

She curtsied deeply and offered her hand to him. "Thank you, kind sir," she said. "I am yours."

"I certainly hope so," was all he said as he led her to the passenger side of the truck.

The Jackpot

"You're catching me pre-caffeinated, so this better be good!" Cathy snarled into the phone. She didn't even bother to lift her head from the pillow.

The incessant ringing had ripped her from a deep slumber, the first full rest she'd had in about three weeks, and she was not impressed.

"Oh sorry, Cathy. Did I wake you?" Cathy winced as Margie Green's high-pitched voice stabbed through her brain.

"Uh-huh." *Now go away.*

"Oh, well, sorry, " Margie said, though Cathy doubted if she was sincere. Margie never seemed too concerned about other people's sensibilities. "I just wanted to call and see if you checked your ticket yet."

"Ticket?" Cathy fought to clear the fog still clouding her thought processes.

"The ticket. You know."

"I do?"

"Oh, come on, Cathy!" Margie laughed.

Cathy gritted her teeth. "Look, Margie. I just did three weeks of almost constant twenty-hour days of inventory. I'm tired, I'm cranky, and I just started a new diet. So unless this is to tell me I won the lottery or something, I'd really appreciate if you would just let—me—sleep!"

"But that's what I'm talking about—" Margie's voice had

risen in volume.

"And that is?" In about five minutes Cathy was going to reach through the phone and rip Miss Peppy-pants' tongue out.

"The lottery!" Margie said. "I heard on the radio this morning that there were two winning tickets for last night's lottery sold in our area. Two point five million dollars! I've been on the phone all morning to everyone from work. I haven't even been out to check my own ticket." A rush of laughter pierced through the line.

"Lottery?" The memory washed over Cathy. A week ago—Margie, another of the librarians blathering on about the size of the jackpot and talking them all into buying tickets. Cathy, irritated at Margie's piercing voice bombarding her, snapping an agreement to just shut her up. "Look, Margie, I never win anything, so thanks for the call, but I'm going back to sleep now."

"Don't forget—" were the last words Cathy heard as she slammed down the receiver.

She rolled heavily over to her other side. She adjusted her ample breasts and belly to a comfortable position and pulled the duvet over her head. If she was lucky, she might just be able to drift off again.

She cursed vehemently as the phone shrilled again. With a violent shrug, she flipped the duvet off and snatched the phone off the cradle.

"What!"

Margie's giggle announced the offender. "I guess we were cut off. I just wanted to say, don't forget to call me when you've checked your ticket. I mean, you could be a millionaire."

"Sure, Margie." Their good-byes said, Cathy reflected that she'd choose the time for her call very carefully. Revenge was sweet.

She lay back down and realized that the time for finding blissful sleep again was gone. With a curse, she pushed herself up to a seated position on the side of the bed. She rubbed her tired eyes and thought about Margie's last words. A millionaire. The thought was appealing. It would be nice to have enough money to perhaps go back to school, or buy a nice home, maybe travel a little. With a sigh, she pushed up to her feet and trudged to the bathroom. It seemed that rather than sleeping the day away, she would be going out to check her ticket.

THE MALL was a busy place, and Cathy had to drive around for several minutes before a convenient parking spot presented itself. It just added fuel to the fire of her frustration. She'd wanted a restful day, and here she was fighting traffic at the mall.

She climbed out of the car and trudged toward the entrance of Stan's Smoke Shop, where she could buy the day's paper. She asked herself again why she was bothering. She never won things. But Margie's words echoed again in her mind—*a millionaire*.

She took the paper to her car. A few minutes of digging through her purse produced the ticket. She thumbed through the paper to the list with the winning numbers, which she compared to her ticket. For several seconds she stared at the two pieces of paper, unable to comprehend fully what she was seeing. Then the realization was a whirling maelstrom in her brain. Her heart raced and the pressure built within her until she let out one great whoop of joy.

"Holy cow," she whispered through the faint echo of her shout.

YET ANOTHER FLASH exploded in Cathy's face, and she grimaced to think what expression the photographer caught. She was so uncomfortable with all the press people clamoring to ask her questions and take her picture. It was a far cry from her quiet little basement office at the library. There she didn't need to worry if her hair was mussed, her makeup was smeared or the extra twenty pounds she'd gained over Christmas was showing. All she needed to do her filing and research was a warm sweater and 20/20 vision.

Cathy took a quick look in the mirror backing the podium where the ceremony was about to take place. Not bad. She hadn't even wanted to come, but Mr. Peabody, the representative from the lottery office, had been firm. To get her check, she had to appear at their ceremony.

So she had splurged a week's pay on a trip to an upscale salon just the day before.

"Oh Madam," the receptionist had gushed. "We will make a totally new woman out of you!"

Cathy had thought wryly that someone *needed* to make a new woman out of her. She wasn't exactly jazzed about the woman she was. But she was also a realist. There would be no silk purse out of this sow's ear.

But she had been pleasantly surprised at the results.

Cathy checked her image once more. She had to admit, she looked good. Her soft ash blonde hair was cut in a cute bob that framed her facial features, making them almost delicate. The skillful but minimal makeup they had taught her to apply made her dark eyes leap from her face and gave her skin a natural, healthy glow.

And the new outfit, a simple floral cotton print princess-line dress, flattered her curves. Instead of feeling dumpy and fat, she felt feminine and curvaceous.

In a few moments, the press conference would begin in earnest. She was curious to meet her fellow prizewinner, a man by the unbelievable name of R.J. Vanderbilt. She'd been told that there was no relation to the illustrious family, but she still thought of him as some stuffy, stuck-up rich kid who didn't need the money anyway.

Reality was far from that image. He turned out to be six foot two of strong, lean he-man. He was dressed in well-worn denim pants and shirt and work boots. His concession to the press conference was a sports coat thrown over his attire. But as he walked through the room, Cathy could hear the palpable sigh emanating from the female members of the crowd as they reacted to his sheer masculinity.

He looked as uncomfortable as Cathy felt. She seemed to relax, feeling a kinship with him. She smiled and caught his eye. He smiled back and Cathy's breath caught in her throat. It wasn't nervousness. It was attraction, pure, animal, and completely new to Cathy.

"Get a grip, old girl," Cathy said to herself. "He's way out of your league."

Cathy became aware suddenly that there was silence and all

eyes turned on her. She realized with a sickening feeling that she had been asked a question and didn't have a clue what it was.

"I beg your pardon?" she said, barely above a whisper. Her amplified voice seemed to shout in her ears.

"Could you tell us how you're feeling at this moment," said a female reporter near the front of the crowd.

"Well," Cathy said with some hesitation. And then she met her co-winner's eyes and felt strangely calmed. "I feel like I just won the jackpot." The warm laughter of the crowd washed over her.

"Mr. Vanderbilt? Do you have anything to add?" All eyes turned to the taciturn man.

"Not really," he began. His voice was like smooth, dark chocolate and sent an additional thrill down Cathy's spine. He then turned and looked deeply into Cathy's eyes.

"I think Miss Merrick said it best." He smiled, causing Cathy to blush. She liked how her name sounded on his tongue.

Moments later the press conference was over, the check presented, the last pictures taken for posterity. And she and R.J. Vanderbilt were alone on the podium.

An awkward silence fell between them. Cathy finally cleared her throat and thrust her hand out. "Hi, I'm Cathy Merrick." Then blushed, realizing he already knew that. She could have kicked herself for acting like some mindless teeny-bopper.

"Ray," he said, giving her hand a firm shake. Such big hands he had.

"Nice to meet you, Ray." To which he nodded assent. Definitely the strong, silent type. The silence widened.

"Well, I guess that's it, then," Cathy said, looking around at the now near-empty room.

"Guess so," Ray mumbled.

Realizing that scintillating conversation was not in the cards, she thrust her hand out again. "Well, congratulations." Another strong handshake and a mumbled "likewise." And then he was gone, leaving Cathy feeling strangely bereft.

"Idiot!" she said, under her breath. She wasn't referring to him.

IT DIDN'T TAKE LONG to slip back into routine after her extraordinary experience. She just stayed down in her little cubby in the basement of the library and quietly did her job. The money was deposited in the bank and earning interest. She had no idea what to do with it, so she just ignored it.

And she was depressed. Whoever said that money couldn't buy happiness was dead to rights. She was really quite miserable, and afraid to look too closely at the cause of her misery. For if she did, she might have to admit that she was lonely.

The loneliness was heightened by her vivid recall of Ray's effect on her respiratory system at the press conference. She'd had her share of romances in her thirty-eight years, but not one of her boyfriends had made her feel that pulse riot she had felt just from Ray's smile.

"You'll never catch a man if you're heavy," her svelte, well-groomed mother had advised her chubby little girl. But at nine and ten and eleven, she hadn't cared.

When her heart had been broken by the cruelties of her peers in high school, her mother had said, "You could lose the weight if you just tried harder. Then you'd have friends. You really do have a pretty face."

How Cathy had learned to hate that phrase. She always heard the "but" that followed. "But the rest of you is so fat and ugly." No one said that, of course. But the implication was there just the same.

As Cathy got older her mother had given up trying to change her daughter, and a frosty truce was reached. It was a relief to be free of the constant attacks on her physical appearance, but it made the loneliness even deeper for Cathy now. There was no one to talk to about these new, startling feelings that Ray had evoked. She became so morose that soon even her coworkers avoided spending time with her. It was just too depressing.

So it was a surprise when Margie sought her out one cold and rainy day. Cathy had been entering new acquisitions into the library computer system. She had been at it for several hours and was almost in a trance-like state. Margie's voice startled her enough that she jumped.

"God, I'm sorry," Margie said. "I didn't mean to scare you."

"That's okay," Cathy said, holding her hand to her chest in an effort to calm her pounding heart. "Can I help you?"

"Well—" Cathy noted the strange expression on Margie's face, as if she held an exquisite secret.

"What's up, Margie?" Cathy said, impatience beginning to appear in her voice.

"There's someone here asking for you," Margie said, almost bouncing with excitement.

"For me?" Cathy was clearly confused. "Who?"

"It's a man!" Margie blurted and grinned.

"Any particular man?" Cathy asked with growing perplexity.

"A *very* particular man," Margie said, drawing out her enjoyment of the moment to its extreme.

Cathy was fast losing her temper. "Well, are you going to tell me who it is, or do we have to have a little game of twenty questions?"

Margie must have sensed the rising anger in Cathy's voice, because she took a deep breath and said, "Ray Vanderbilt!"

Cathy was stunned. Ray was here? But why? It had been two weeks since the press conference and not a word. Why was he seeking her out now? There must be some kind of problem with the money. But then, why wouldn't Mr. Peabody be calling? It just didn't make sense.

"Where?" was all she could choke. Her eyes pleaded with Margie to just understand. Strangely enough, she seemed to.

"I took him to the lunchroom. I'll make sure everyone stays away and gives you two privacy." Taking Cathy's hands in hers, she grinned and said, "Good luck."

Good luck. Why would she need good luck? It wasn't as if anything could happen between her and Ray, after all. But despite this surety she took a moment to stop in the ladies room and check her hair and straighten her clothing. She stared at herself in the mirror and saw fevered eyes and fear. What would Ray see?

His back was to the door when Cathy walked into the lunch-room. She took a moment to pause and take a deep, calming breath.

"Hello Ray," she said, glad that her voice didn't tremble. "This is a surprise."

He jumped to his feet, and Cathy could swear that he was just as nervous as she was.

"Yeah, I guess it is," he said, thrusting his hand out. "How have you been?"

She shook his hand. Was it her imagination, or did he hold on for a beat longer than usual?

"I'm good," she lied. "Nothing has changed at all." Another lie. "All that money doesn't seem quite real."

"I know what you mean," Ray said, as they both took a chair. "I went back to the construction site right after the press conference. It just didn't feel right not to keep going to work every day."

"Exactly," Cathy said vehemently, then sank into silence.

Ray looked thoughtful and then nodded as if making a deci-sion.

"I guess you're wondering why I'm here." He stood and began to pace the length of the little lunchroom. He ran a slightly trem-bling hand through his hair.

"A little."

"I'm a pretty quiet-living guy, Cathy. I like my job. I like to play pick-up games of baseball with some buddies on the weekends. I like to mess around on my guitar, but I'm not very good."

Cathy smiled her understanding.

"What I'm trying to say is, I'm not someone who goes around looking for the high life. My buddies think I'm a little strange, I think, that I don't run around with lots of girls, being single and all. And my mother long ago gave up on me ever giving her grandkids, but to tell you the truth, it was just important for me to find the right person."

"I understand," Cathy said. She gave a little laugh, "at least about my mother giving up on me, too."

Ray stopped pacing and sat, leaning his elbows on his knees

and concentrating on his clenched fists. Cathy swallowed the apprehension in her throat.

"Something happened the day of the press conference," he said to his fists.

"Oh?"

"I don't want you to think I'm weird or anything. But, I just sensed some chemistry here." Cathy's gasp brought his eyes up to hers. "Am I wrong?"

"I—I—"She was stunned.

Ray jumped to his feet and started pacing again.

"I knew it. You think I'm weird. I don't blame—"

"No!" Cathy said. "Please sit down. You're making me a little dizzy pacing like that. I don't think you're weird. I'm just not sure what you mean."

"Nothing out of line," Ray replied. "I just mean that we seemed to connect. You're not what I expected you to be."

"Oh?"

"Yeah, I expected some supermarket tabloid type, all tight pants and teased hair."

Cathy laughed. "I thought you'd be some overbearing Wall Street type."

"I guess we were both mistaken." Cathy liked his laugh. "I'm glad you're just a nice, pretty girl."

Cathy wasn't sure she'd heard him right. He'd called her pretty. A warm glow started to grow in the center of her chest. And just as quickly a cold chill replaced it. This was some sort of joke or setup. Good looking guys did not track her down and call her pretty. It just wasn't something that happened to chubby girls.

"Look, who sent you?"

Ray stared at her, not comprehending.

"What?"

"Look, it's okay. I understand. Someone set you up to do this. Probably Margie. This is her kind of thing. Well, thanks, but no thanks." She stood, making it clear their time was up.

Ray slowly rose, anger visible on his face.

"That's quite a chip you have there," he said dryly.

"Chip? What chip?"

"The huge one you're struggling under with regard to your looks."

"What would you know about it?" Cathy was getting angry herself.

"I know it's so huge that it blocks your view of what's in front of you."

"And that is?"

"Someone who finds you very attractive despite the disfiguring chip you carry."

And he turned and walked out of the room. For once in her life Cathy was at a loss for words. For about the space of three heartbeats.

"Wait!"

She rushed through the door only to find her way obstructed by a broad chest and a pair of crossed arms. Ray hadn't left. He'd waited for her to come to her senses. Her heart sang.

"Can I just try that once more?"

"All but that last couple of minutes." The beginnings of a smile twitched at the corner of his mouth.

Cathy raised her hand to her shoulder and with exaggerated force, flicked an imaginary object from her shoulder.

"That feels better," she said, with an equally exaggerated sigh.

"Looks better, too." Ray was grinning now. "Let me repeat myself. I'm glad you're just a nice, pretty girl."

"Me too. I mean, I'm glad you're a nice guy."

"I almost didn't go to the press conference at all. I didn't even want the damn money. The ticket was a gift from my brother for my birthday." He shook his head. "What I'm trying to say is, I never realized that I was missing anything in my life until that day."

"Oh?" An inkling of understanding was dawning in Cathy's mind.

"But I'm so glad I went," he said, smiling warmly at Cathy. Her heart responded by skipping a beat.

"You are?" she said, her voice barely audible.

"Yes," said Ray softly. "Because I met you."

"Oh, my." All Cathy could seem to do was grin and blush.

"And I've been thinking a lot about you this past two weeks, trying to work up the courage to track you down and ask you out."

"Oh, my!"

"So I wondered if I might take you out for a coffee so we could get acquainted." Ray chuckled. "I think I can afford it."

Cathy laughed, too, and was surprised to find that her heart felt unusually light. "I'd love to."

"Great!" Ray said, standing and offering his hand to a bemused Cathy. "Then I guess I really did hit the jackpot."

Wrong Number?

*L*ori yawned and stretched her now tired and resistant muscles. She was seven hours into the night shift at the answering service, and the strain was beginning to show. The 11–7 shift seemed long at the best of times, but tonight it seemed endless. Her mind drifted, as it always seemed to these days, to Dan Raeburn. Just his name gave her a thrill. She felt herself flush, and smiled. If only he were here right now, she would—

A loud buzz sounded on her board, jerking her back to reality.

"Blast it! Why is it that every nut in the city seems to know when I'm working?" she muttered to herself. It was a holiday weekend, a time in itself that would guarantee an overactive switchboard, but add a waxing full moon and it was no-holds-barred at the funny farm.

She saw that it was Dr. Abrams's line. "Great. This ought to be good."

Dr. Abrams was a therapist. His patients tended to be skittish at the best of times. She couldn't imagine what might transpire on a night like this.

"Dr. Abrams's answering service," she answered in her usual smooth, professional voice.

"Hello? Hello?" A strident and horribly familiar voice came across the wire. "I need to talk to the doctor."

"This is Dr. Abrams's answering service." Lori marveled once again at how the general public seemed to think that doctors kept 24–7 hours. And this woman was the worst. She had been calling at the same time every week for the past six weeks. Lori fought to keep civil. "May I please take a message?"

There was a slight pause. "I gotta talk to him right now! Tell him it's Millie."

"Dr. Abrams's office is closed on Sundays, ma'am. This is his answering service. May I take a message?"

"It's an emergency!"

Right, thought Lori, *you need an emergency consult with your therapist at 6:30 in the morning.* It was the same routine every time. "Ma'am, it's Sunday." Lori fought to keep her voice calm.

"No, it's not!" was the rude response.

Lori gritted her teeth. Right on cue! "Yes ma'am, it is Sunday. Dr. Abrams's office will open tomorrow morning at 8 a.m."

"I think I know what day it is!" The voice was whining now, setting Lori's teeth on edge.

She took a deep breath and began again. "Ma'am? I don't work on Mondays. It *is* Sunday. Now, Dr. Abrams is not avail—"

"I heard you!" said the voice rudely. "I'm sure it's Monday. It wouldn't hurt you to get him for me, would it?"

Lori's self-control snapped. Enough of being polite. Enough of offering her a referral to the on-call physician, which she would turn down anyway. Enough! "Ma'am? Do you have cable television?"

There was a pause, then, "Yes."

"Are you near your TV set?"

"Yes."

"Turn it on and tune into the TV guide channel."

"Okay."

"Now, look at the bottom righthand corner and see the date. What does it say?"

"Sunday."

"Now, ma'am," Lori's voice was tight. "Do you believe the cable company knows what day it is?"

"Yes."

"Good! You can reach Dr. Abrams TOMORROW morning!" Lori disconnected the line and leaned back tiredly in her chair. "Will this night ever be over?"

Another buzz sounded. "Oh, what now!" She smiled when she saw which line it was. "Raeburn Computers. May I take a message?"

"Hey, dollface! How's my favorite operator?" A surge of energy went through Lori. It was Dan.

"Well, hi Dan, how are you? Better yet, where are you?"

"I'm good, doll, but a little tired. I'm in Moosejaw and just got up to get ready for a big pow-wow with a new client. And I was with this client until 2 this morning, so I haven't had much shut-eye."

"You poor baby," Lori purred. She was reveling in the deep, sexy tones of Dan's voice. She could listen to him forever.

"I'm so touched you care, dollface. I just have to get him signed on the dotted line, iron out some details, and I should be able to be home by late tomorrow."

"You work too hard, Dan," Lori said in a motherly fashion, feeling not in the least like a mother. "You need to stop and smell the roses once in a while."

"Honey," he chuckled, "nobody ever got rich from smelling roses!"

"Money isn't everything," Lori said. "What about love? A family?"

"Hey, to use operator parlance, all my romances turn out to be wrong numbers. Besides, I'm saving myself for you, dollface," Dan said, his low chuckle again sending a rush of delicious sensation down Lori's spine.

"Talk, talk, talk," Lori chided. "Talk is cheap, buddy!"

"Ouch," Dan said. "One of these days, doll, one of these days. Say, are there any messages for me?"

It was always like this. A little banter, some light flirtation, and then business as usual. Lori figured that Dan was probably the gun-shy type.

Dan Raeburn had been a client of the answering service for

over two years, and for over two years Lori and Dan had engaged in this playful verbal jousting. They had become friends of a sort and probably knew more about each other than their other friends did. The unique aspect of their friendship was that they had never met.

That was partly because of strict rules the answering service had against meeting with clients. Lori knew that some of the other operators had bent that rule from time to time, but she had never strayed, a fact she regretted more and more when it came to Dan.

He was wonderful, warm and funny, caring and sweet. He had intelligence and ambition, charm and good taste. His voice was deep and rich, a baritone that sent thrills through Lori every time she heard it. In her mind she had concocted a picture to match that voice. He was probably tall and broad shouldered. She imagined hair that fell over his brow in a boyish fashion. She could also imagine her fingers lifting that hair to kiss the brow beneath. He would dress well, in clothes that would enhance his muscular build. But best of all, his eyes—his eyes would be deep and expressive, so deep that she could drown in them.

Give your head a shake, Lori my girl, she said to herself after she had passed on Dan's messages and he had signed off. *No guy like that is going to go for a girl like you.*

Not that there was anything inherently wrong with Lori's looks, but she had always had the feeling that she was rather ordinary. She was about average height by most standards, at 5 feet 5. She had a nice enough figure, but by popular tastes she was too heavy; chunky, her brother called her. Her legs were shapely and she liked to show them off, but the rest of her body she tried to disguise. Her hair was her best feature by far, being a wonderful rich auburn that curled naturally around her expressive face. And her warm brown eyes danced with humor and intelligence that could not be ignored. But like many women, she wished for features other than her own, thinking they would be more desirable to someone like Dan.

She had never told Dan that she was a big girl. It was probably better that they remain faceless friends. There was no chance of disappointment then.

These thoughts were still running around in her head two days later when Dan called once again.

"Hey, dollface!"

That same thrill went through Lori. She really liked this man. "Hi, Dan. No messages for you tonight, my friend," Lori replied.

"Well, actually," Dan began, stammering a little, which was so unusual for the usually glib man. "I didn't call tonight for my messages."

"Okay, I'll bite," Lori quipped. "Why did you call? Bored with watching TV in your hotel room?"

"Actually—" Again he seemed to hesitate. "Actually, I'm home."

Lori's heart skipped a beat. He never called the service when he was in town. He didn't need to.

"That's nice," she said cautiously. "You needed to stop and get some rest."

"Well, that, too," Dan said cryptically. "Look, I'm stumbling all over myself here. The reason I called was to ask you—to see if—I wondered if you might—Sheesh! Why is this so hard? Look, will you come and have a coffee with me this morning." The last part came out in a long rush, punctuated by a big sigh at the end and then silence.

Lori sat frozen, unable to comprehend what she had just heard. Dan was asking her out?

"Lori? Are you there?" The worried tone in Dan's voice brought Lori out of her stupor.

"Uh, yeah, Dan, I'm here," Lori stammered. "I'm just not sure I heard you right."

"I just asked you out," Dan said, his tone still apprehensive. "You, um, don't sound too enthused. Did I get another 'wrong number?'"

Lori smiled. Even nervous, he could crack a joke. "No, of course not, you just took me by surprise, that's all."

"I thought I wouldn't give you a chance to think about it too much, in case you decided no."

"I see." Lori couldn't keep the smile out of her voice.

"It's been on my mind for a while, you know, asking you out," Dan said. "I really enjoy our talks on the phone. In fact, I look forward to them."

Lori's heart was pounding. He had been thinking of her. He had wanted to ask her out.

"Look, you probably have rules about not dating clients," Dan said, "but could you make an exception in this case?" Lori didn't give herself time to think twice. As long as she didn't get caught—

"Um, Dan, before I answer, I have something to tell you."

"Oh?" He sounded guarded.

Lori took a deep breath and plunged ahead. "There's something you need to know about me."

"What? You have some weird hang-up or quirk I don't know about?" He chuckled at his own wit.

"Something like that. Look, you should know I'm a little on the chubby side."

"So?" He hadn't even missed a beat.

"You don't mind?" Lori held her breath.

"It's not what's on the outside that matters. And what I know of what you have on the inside is pretty special."

"Wow."

"So, is that it?"

Lori laughed. "That's it."

"So, coffee?"

"I'd love to," she said, sounding breathless.

"Great!" Relief was palpable in Dan's voice. "So when do you get off?"

"Seven," Lori said. She suddenly felt depressed. It would probably be too early. He'd change his mind once he thought about things. She shouldn't have gotten her hopes—

"Super!"

Super? Had she heard right?

Dan continued, "I can pick you up or we can meet at the Dandy Donuts over on First Street."

"I know the place," Lori said. "It's about three blocks from my work. Why don't I meet you there?"

"Great! It's a date."

A date. A date with Dan! Lori's head was spinning. She heard a chuckle. "What's so funny?" she asked.

"I guess I should ask you what you look like—besides, you know," Dan said.

"Oh, yeah." Lori joined in the laughter. "I suppose that would help. 5-5, brown hair, brown eyes, wearing jeans and a cable-knit sweater. Pretty ordinary."

"I'll be the judge of that, dollface," Dan quipped. "See you just after seven." And then the line was dead.

Lori sat for the longest time staring at the wall before the ramifications of the phone call hit her. "Oh my God, have I completely lost my mind?"

By the end of her shift, Lori was a complete emotional wreck. She had made error after error, something she normally wouldn't have done. She felt wound up like a coiled spring and about ready to explode. And here she was minutes away from her date and she was questioning her sanity at accepting the invitation.

Walking out of the answering service was like emerging from a cave. The sun was still low in the sky and the city was still relatively quiet. Lori took a deep breath to calm her nerves. As she pulled out of her parking spot, she wondered if she should just turn toward home and forget the whole thing.

"Okay, Lori girl," she muttered. "You've been dreaming of this forever, so don't chicken out now. What's the worst thing that can happen?" She didn't really want to think about it.

BUSINESS WAS GETTING BRISK at Dandy Donuts. Everyone was getting his or her morning fix of caffeine and sugar. Lori's heart beat an erratic rhythm as she sat watching person after person enter or emerge from the coffee shop. She was shaking and sure that her legs wouldn't support her. Again, her inner voice pricked at her. *Go now or forever hold your peace.*

The comforting smell of good coffee as she entered the door helped her get a grip on herself, and she scanned the room in search of Dan. Several people were lined up at the counter. None appeared to fit her mental picture of him. The few tables were occupied, but again, none seemed to be waiting for anyone. Then a panicking thought came into her mind. What if Dan had changed his mind? What if he didn't show up? She hadn't considered that. Or what if he had shown up, waited in his car, seen her and then changed his mind? That didn't even bear consideration.

Lori sensed someone coming in the door behind and prepared to move out of the way.

"I don't suppose it's you, dollface," said a deep, sexy and very familiar voice.

"Dan?" Lori heard the quaver in her voice and cleared her throat as she slowly turned around.

"In the flesh!" Warm, dark eyes twinkled down at her, tiny creases at the outer corner testimony to how often he smiled. His face was split into a boyish grin and Lori wanted so much to gently smooth the unruly lock of curly brown hair that fell onto his forehead.

His tall, trim frame looked wonderful in jeans, golf shirt and a well-cut leather jacket. In one hand was a single red rose, in the other, a small bouquet of balloons. He chuckled as he saw her eyes take in the balloons.

"I didn't want you to miss me," he said. Then his eyes did their own scrutiny of her. "You're every bit as lovely as I knew you would be."

Lori knew then that she was lost. Whatever doubts she had regarding her job or this man were swept away by those special words.

"So you don't think this was a wrong number?" she said playfully as they took a seat at the nearest table.

He laughed, a sound that warmed her very soul.

"No," he said, and took her hand in his. "This time I think the operator helped me reach the right party."

Vivian's Muse

*V*ivian McLeish would have given anything for her first meeting with Rolly Stevenson not to have included the humiliation of her vomiting the entire contents of her stomach into the bushes.

"Are you all right?" he asked with genuine concern.

Do I look all right? had been her thought, but her actual response had been another violent upsurge from her gut. *Please God, just let me die now.*

"The road certainly is hilly and winding," Rolly said. He took her arm and guided her to the willow chair on the deck.

Thanks for stating the obvious, she wanted to say. But Vivian felt all wobbly and weak, as if her bones had turned to rubber. Her mouth was revolting with the aftertaste of regurgitated breakfast, and her embarrassment would not allow her to look Rolly in the face.

"I'm so sorry you had to witness that," she said instead, her voice as unsteady as her knees. "It's been years since I've come to the cabin. I'd forgotten the effect that road had on me. I'll be okay in a minute."

"No rush, Miss—McLeish, isn't it?"

"Uh-huh."

"Rolly. Rolly Stevenson." He stood there, and Vivian sensed she was expected to say something. She braved a look. Workboots, denim jeans, plaid shirt, nice smile, peaked cap with a beer logo. She went back to the smile and attempted a wan smile in return.

Figures, she thought. "Can I help you with something?" She didn't know what, since it was she, in her city suit and leather pumps, who was the stranger. Rolly looked puzzled.

"I was hired to open up the cabin and make sure it was ready for you."

"Oh, my PA must have called you."

"I wouldn't know about that, but anyway, I knew you were arriving this morning and thought I'd be here to show you around."

"That's nice, but not necessary. I came here every summer for years when I was a kid. My fondest memories are of this lake."

"Well, it hasn't changed much since then, I'm sure. Why'd you stop coming?"

"Look, Rolly," Vivian said with impatience. "I don't mean to be rude, but I don't really feel up to a friendly *tete-a-tete* at the moment. So if you don't mind—" She stood up for emphasis.

Rolly's cheeks reddened slightly and his relaxed stance vanished. "Oh, sure, no problem. I just thought—See you, then."

"Thanks." Vivian watched as he climbed into his half-ton and drove out the lane. She felt a momentary twinge of regret at being so abrupt with the man. He had seemed quite nice. But damn it! She had come here to get away from people, to have some long-needed peace and quiet. Her next desire was to rid her mouth of the sour acid aftertaste of her unfortunate episode.

She stood for a moment and drank in lungfuls of cool, clean air. Yes, maybe here she would at last reclaim her self and reconnect with the creative muse that had deserted her.

ROLLY FUMED, his foot pressed hard on the gas, and the rear end of his truck fishtailed in protest. Common sense overrode anger and he slowed down.

What a snob she was. A big-shot writer with a big city attitude, she'd acted like she was so high and mighty. Well, she's human like the rest of us. He relished the picture of her hunkered over the bushes retching up her last meal. How the mighty had fallen!

And then Rolly slammed on the brakes and pulled to the shoulder, wrenching the gearshift to park. The truck rocked slightly with the violence of the action.

"What's really bothering you, old man?" Rolly asked his reflection in the rearview mirror. And there it was. He was a fan of Vivian McLeish. He'd read every one of her medical thrillers. When he'd gotten the call from her assistant asking him to get the old McLeish property fit for her residence, he'd been filled with such an eagerness to meet her.

When she stumbled out of her car and was so violently ill, he had felt such compassion. Even in such an awkward circumstance, he had noticed her voluptuous good looks. She was a subject worthy of an artist like Rubens, who had glorified the fuller figure.

Rolly couldn't help but be struck by the sun picking out the glints of gold in her bronze-colored curls and the thickness of the lashes that had framed her piercing green eyes. Her voice had been deep and rich, so sexy to his ear. His middle-aged heart had done a serious hop, skip and jump and he had trouble getting a coherent thought together. He was just trying to make some pleasant conversation, and she had treated him like some pesky country rube.

Well, screw her! He slammed the truck back in gear and with a very satisfying scatter of gravel drove on. He sure as hell would think twice before offering the hand of friendship to Vivian McLeish again!

By NIGHTFALL Vivian was truly exhausted, but in that pleasant way that speaks of jobs accomplished and a rest well-earned.

She had stowed her gear and had a thorough tour through all the rooms and cupboards of the cabin. One thing she could say for Mr. Stevenson, he had been thorough in his preparations. The cabin was clean and well-stocked with food. She would only need a quick trip to town for a few perishables. A fire had been laid in the wood stove, and there was plenty of wood to keep her going for a few days. He had even been thoughtful enough to air out one of the bedrooms and have it ready for immediate use. A lovely vase of wildflowers was an added welcome.

She had turned the other bedroom into her temporary office with her computer equipment and research materials. But, she wondered wryly, would she be able to make use of them?

Vivian sat curled on the sofa, sipping a glass of Sambuca liqueur and watching the flames dancing in the fireplace. She felt a contentment that had been missing from her life for a long time.

Where had it gone wrong? Success had come swiftly with the release of her first book. She really hadn't had the long years of working and waiting that most writers talk about. She had hit her first time to bat. A phenomenon, the papers called her. Success followed success and ten years passed, a heady whirlwind of promotional tours and book signings, talk shows and even a stint as writer-in-residence at a major university. She had never married, content to let her muse be her companion.

She couldn't really pinpoint when she had become aware of a discontent that invaded all the nooks and crannies of her life. But one day she had awakened to find that her muse, for so long a constant and faithful friend, had deserted her. And with it gone, she was truly alone.

"Why did you never marry?" her agent had asked one day not long ago.

"Oh, I just never met the right one," had been Vivian's glib reply. In truth, she had been afraid; afraid that no one would love her, afraid she wasn't pretty enough or thin enough, afraid to fail.

Unbidden, Rolly Stevenson's kind face floated into her mind. A wash of shame filled Vivian. He had just tried to be helpful and kind and she had rebuffed him like a pesky child.

You'll always be alone, if that's how you treat people, she chided herself. And suddenly she didn't want to be alone. She watched the flames flicker and dance and felt hope.

"IT'S VERY HARD for me to admit I've acted like a spoiled child," Vivian said. She brushed an imaginary speck from the railing of the deck.

Rolly stood by his truck, resolute in his determination not to back down from further attacks from this woman. She stood rigidly uncomfortable on the bottom step.

"I've always been pretty independent," she continued, "but I'm realizing that I need to let others help me. You were so kind to do all you did to the cabin. Please accept my apology and my thanks."

Silence stretched between them, and Vivian began to feel uncomfortable. As it stretched further, she felt anger building. Damn it! She had apologized. What more did the man want?"Look, I'm trying—"

"Apology accepted."

"—to say I'm sorry. What?"

Rolly scuffed the gravel with the toe of his boot. "Apology accepted." He smiled tentatively.

Vivian smiled back. How could she have forgotten what a nice smile he had? "Thank you for all you did around here to make me welcome."

"It was nothing, really." He seemed about to say something else, paused, then blurted. "I've read all your books."

"Have you really?" Her voice cooled. She inwardly cringed. This was what she was trying to get away from, this fawning at her celebrity. Rolly wasn't stupid. He sensed her retreat.

"I expect you get that a lot," he said. He shifted his weight uncomfortably.

"Some," she answered. Her arms were crossed, an unconscious shield erected.

"Damn! Me and my big mouth!" Gravel scattered from the impact of his boot.

Vivian thawed, amused at the picture of "little boy" contrition that the middle-aged Rolly presented. Her body relaxed and she smiled warmly.

Rolly's reaction to that smile was a momentary loss of his ability to breathe.

"Don't be silly," she said, a chuckle chasing her words. "I have to be less suspicious and just learn to accept a compliment."

Rolly took a step or two toward Vivian. Their eyes locked, and for a moment the natural sounds of birds, rustling leaves and lapping water faded, and the two were aware only of their rapidly beating hearts.

"Um—" Rolly said, breaking the spell with that syllable. "I really do enjoy your books. You're a wonderful writer."

"Thank you," Vivian replied. She felt herself blush. "Does your—um—wife—also read my books?" And her blush deepened as she realized how this must sound.

Rolly grinned, not fooled at all. "I'm divorced," he said. "Have been for almost ten years."

"I'm sorry," she said.

"Don't be. I'm not." He was standing quite close now. She could see the shadow of stubble on his chin and the smattering of gray at his temples. "And you?"

"What?" Startled, she blinked, trying hard to remember what was being discussed. "Oh. No. I mean—I've never been married—other than to my work." She grimaced. When did she start to sound like an idiot? "Um—Mr. Stevenson?"

"Rolly."

"Uh, Rolly? Would you care to come in and have a cup of coffee?"

Rolly grinned broadly. "I would, indeed."

VIVIAN SIGNED the last page of the contract with a flourish and sat back contentedly.

"Vivian, *The Handyman's Heart* is going to be a blockbuster!" her publisher beamed.

"Thanks, Hal," Vivian said. "I have to admit, it was my favorite book to write."

"It shows. It's an unusual departure for you, going from thriller to romance, but it's such a compelling story. I think your readers will eat it up. I see it as the start of a whole new phase of your writing career."

"Perhaps," Vivian said. "We'll see what the muse brings on next. But for the time being, I have more important things to focus on."

"More important than your writing?" Hal said. Vivian laughed at his genuine alarm.

"Hal, dear," she said. "My husband and I deserve to have a honeymoon. The poor man has been incredibly patient while I finished *The Handyman's Heart*. I've promised to take some time off."

"How is Rolly?"

Vivian's face broke into a radiant smile. "He's wonderful!" she said, sighing. "He's almost got the new cabin finished. It's absolutely gorgeous! We begin work on the rest of the writer's retreat after we have our honeymoon."

"It's a wonderful idea, you know," Hal said, "providing a getaway so writers can get their creative juices going again."

"It was Rolly's idea," Vivian said proudly. "He saw what being at the cabin did for my own creativity. Of course, he fails to see the influence he had in the whole process." She grinned. "Being in love is a wonderful source of inspiration."

"That it is," Hal said, picking up the contract Vivian had just signed. "May the inspiration never end."

Amen to that, Vivian thought. With hope and happiness and her wonderful husband as her guides, she was sure it never would.

Belle's Jingle

$\mathcal{B}$elle Stephens cranked up the volume on the car radio. As she heard the familiar tune of the commercial her heart pounded.

"Deck the halls, the time is right. For using Russco's Shines So Bright." The trio of female singers ended and a melodic, rather seductive voice added, "The cleanser with the holiday spirit."

Belle grinned with pride as she listened to the jingle that won Wakefield Industry's Holiday Ad Contest. The jingle she had composed.

She'd done it as a dare to herself. Writing ever since she could hold a pencil, she'd only begun this year, after her thirty-fifth birthday, to pursue it seriously. This contest was her first foray into the real world of publishing—a chance to get some recognition and if lucky, pocket the $500 cash prize and receive a new laptop.

She was astounded when the letter arrived informing her that she'd bagged the first prize. And now her little jingle was being played on the air, and it filled her with euphoria every time she heard it.

Traffic came to a halt at an intersection and Belle took the opportunity to glance at her reflection in the rearview mirror. Excitement had brought an attractive blush of color to her normally pale complexion. Her light green eyes danced with delight, and she noticed that she wore the same Mona Lisa smile that seemed a permanent fixture these days. Running her fingers through her thick, shoulder-length chestnut brown hair, she made a mental note to get a trim soon and maybe look at a whole new style to mark the start of her writing career.

She chuckled to herself at the notion of a writing career. She was hardly ready to give up her day job. There would be many more years of private piano lessons given to reluctant grade-schoolers, and tedious courses in music theory taught at the local conservatory, before she could chuck it all in for the gypsy life of a writer.

Traffic started to creep along again, and Belle began looking for a parking spot. She was a bit nervous about meeting with Russell Wakefield, CEO of Wakefield Industries, tonight at the very prestigious Le Gourmand restaurant. He would present her with her check and laptop and treat her to a gourmet meal. A car pulled out just down the block. Luck sided with Belle, and left the spot open for her to park the Jeep.

She mentally surveyed herself. At five foot five and a plump 190 pounds, she'd long ago given up hope of ever looking like the svelte, leggy fashion models whose figures she'd always envied. Upon hitting her thirties, she also came to the realization that she'd better darn well make the most of what God had given her, or spend her life in misery—a fate her natural *joie de vivre* wouldn't allow. So with that in mind, she'd started acquiring a wardrobe that was steps above the serviceable camouflage to which she'd been accustomed. Tonight she chose a smart pantsuit in a shade of emerald green that particularly flattered her coloring. The slight flair in the pant-leg and the clever tailoring of the jacket gave her figure the illusion of more height. A soft silk camisole peeked out at the top of her jacket, adding femininity to the ensemble.

Her grandmother's emerald studs nestled in her ears and gave her courage. Nana Annabelle would have been so proud of her namesake.

BELLE EXPERIENCED another pang of panic when she walked into the packed restaurant. The wall of shoulders and backs in the line-up in front of her obscured her view. How would she ever find

Mr. Wakefield in this mob, short of pole-vaulting onto the maitre d's little desk? That thought cheered her immensely, and as if by magic, the bodies in front of her disappeared and the maitre d' offered to guide her to Mr. Wakefield's table.

Contrary to Belle's expectations, Mr. Wakefield turned out to be young, tall and terribly good-looking. The dazzling combination was enough to render Belle mute on the spot.

Good-looking guys had always had that effect on Belle. She'd never considered herself to be in the running for their attentions—especially if there were taller, slimmer girls around. She assumed men were more interested in that lithe, willowy type. After all, wasn't that the image she saw every time she opened a magazine or turned on the television? Years of experience had served to make her rather touchy about the whole subject.

Russ Wakefield stood and offered his hand. "You must be Annabelle Stephens."

Belle could only nod as she stared and limply shook his hand.

"Russ Wakefield. I'm pleased to meet you, and have to tell you that I was really impressed with your jingle."

"Thank you." Belle sat across from this unexpected vision. "I hope you won't think me rude, but you're *much* younger than I expected you to be."

Russ laughed and nodded. "I get that reaction all the time. You were no doubt expecting Russell Wakefield, my grandfather. He's CEO of Wakefield Industries. I'm named after him. My Dad got dubbed Junior, much to his chagrin, and I answer to Russ, to avoid confusion. I'm V.P. in charge of Public Relations. Granddad believes in nepotism tempered with a strong work ethic."

Belle smiled and nodded with understanding. "My Nana Annabelle was the same way. She'd often say, 'anything worth having is worth working for.'"

"Sounds like my Granddad. You're named after her,, then?"

"Yep." Belle smiled as she fingered the emerald earrings. "She's gone now, but she's never far away in spirit."

The waiter came and took their drink orders. They laughed when they both asked for a dry white wine spritzer with a twist of lime, and a bond of warmth was forged between them.

"So, do you look like your grandmother?" Russ asked, with genuine interest in his eyes.

"Short and stocky," Belle replied glibly. "That was Nana, and as you can see, that's me, too." She endeavored to keep her quip light, but there was an edge of self-consciousness there, too. Russ didn't seem to notice.

"You have unusual eyes." His intent gaze made Belle uncomfortable. "They seem the color of emeralds."

Belle shrugged. "My Dad used to call me the green-eyed monster," she said. She heard her own nervous twitter and mentally kicked herself to chill out. "I was a bit of a brat as a child, I'm afraid."

"Looks like you turned out all right in the end," Russ said.

Belle couldn't be sure, but it seemed as if he was flirting with her. Flirting? Couldn't be. Men didn't flirt with her—especially men that looked like Russ Wakefield.

"My Dad might argue with you about that," Belle joked, as she always did when she was uncomfortable. She also hoped that it would cover her discomfort at the intensity of his scrutiny and the unreadable thoughts behind his eyes. "I have a heck of a temper still."

Fortunately the waiter arrived to take their order. They spent the next hour and a half talking about her job and her writing aspirations and what had led to the writing of the jingle. Then she learned about Russ's family business and his close relationship with his grandfather. It had been Russ's idea to run the contest.

"Granddad is pretty conservative in most things and thought that the contest was pretty radical. But we had over 1200 entries and our sales went through the roof for over two weeks. Now he's a little more open to some of the other innovative advertising ideas I have."

"1200 entries!" Belle's fork fell with a clatter to her plate. She was stunned. "I had no idea!"

A broad smile spread across Russ's features. "Well, yours really stood out, Belle. Obviously, because you're the winner. Speaking of which—" He took an envelope out of his suit jacket pocket and handed it to her, and then lifted a rather heavy package from beside his chair. "Here's your check and the laptop. Congratulations."

"Thank you," she said, running her hands over the silver-wrapped box. "And dinner was excellent. I really appreciate all this fuss. I don't often get a treat like this."

"Well, to be honest," Russ said, his intense gaze returning to her face and his body leaning into his words. "Dinner actually wasn't part of the bargain. I kind of threw that in for my own benefit."

Confused, Belle slanted him a puzzled look. "I'm not quite sure what you're saying."

"Well—"

As Russ began to speak, Belle noticed that he looked a little embarrassed and ill at ease. For some reason this alarmed her.

"I was one of the contest judges," Russ continued. "When I saw your picture and bio, I just knew I had to meet you and get to know you a little better. I suppose you could say your picture spoke to me. So, I, um, volunteered to deliver the prizes, and I just quietly added this nice dinner to give us some time to get acquainted."

"You what?" Belle was stunned. Her mind refused to comprehend what this man was apparently saying. It couldn't be true—her ears must be playing tricks on her. Yes, that's it. She'd been alone too long and in her loneliness she was hallucinating the whole scenario.

"You see," Russ went on, unaware of how shaken Belle was, "when I saw your picture, I said to myself, 'wow, this is a girl that I just have to meet. She's lovely!'"

"Me? Lovely?" And she snorted a laugh, making it clear that she found his statement ludicrous. The man actually had the nerve to sit right across from her and ridicule her.

"You seemed surprised." Russ realized that Belle was getting angry when she should be feeling flattered, and it bewildered him.

"No," Belle said, her mind clearing as she made sense of his comments. "I've been the butt of jokes before and I will be again, no doubt. But I must say yours wins the prize for the most creative and cruel. Thank you for delivering my prizes. I'll say good night now. And, Mr. Wakefield, you can go straight to hell."

Belle walked out of the restaurant with quiet dignity. She didn't even turn at his sputtered, "No! Belle, you don't understand."

But she understood all right. Like an idiot, she'd walked right into it and had her heart stomped again. By thirty-five, you think she would have better radar.

The ride home was a blur of tears and angry recriminations. If she could have, she would have spit nails.

So much for the illustrious start of her writing career.

THE NEXT MORNING she slept late, which was unusual for her. It was her habit to rise with the birds and enjoy her two cups of Columbian coffee along with the latest mystery she was reading. However, her night's slumber had been broken by dreams of a handsome, mocking face and bitter laughter.

She'd wake in a sweat, pound her pillows in frustration, and try to find another position where she could fall asleep again. When she woke just before noon, she had a raging headache and a mood to match. The doorbell rang and she strode to take her frustration out on the hapless soul who had broken her peace.

She opened the door to be faced with the largest, most glorious potted poinsettia that she had ever seen. Attached to it was a freckle-faced teenage delivery boy, who nervously thrust the plant into her hands and wordlessly fled back to his florist van.

For a moment she stood immobile in her doorway, until a blast of December air reminded her that she was standing there in just her flannel pajamas and bare feet. She took the plant into her sunny kitchen. It was then that she noticed a small note tucked in the midst of the scarlet blossoms. Curiosity made her clumsy, and she cursed as she finally tore open the tiny envelope.

A token of apology for whatever I might have said to offend you. For what it's worth, I am a sincere guy and meant every word that I said. Best wishes for a joyful holiday season. I wish we'd had more time.

Russ

Belle plopped heavily into one of the kitchen chairs and stared at his words.

Could she possibly have misinterpreted things? Was her radar really that far off? Had she become so suspicious and paranoid that she'd hurt a genuinely nice man showing an honest interest in her?

She went over every moment of the dinner and weighed each word, each gesture and nuance again. In the end, with these gorgeous blossoms to support her new findings, she realized that she'd been wrong—terribly, shamefully wrong.

Misery washed over her like a dank cloud. She was certain that she'd completely burned this particular bridge behind her. Her rash, rude dismissal of Russ would be a sour taste she'd have to swallow each time she recalled the incident.

The phone startled her with its shrill ring and she quickly answered it, glad of the distraction from her wretchedness.

"Hello?"

"Hello, Annabelle. It's Russ."

Her heart hammered in her chest. A ray of hope pierced the dark cloud in her mind.

"I just received the poinsettia. It's absolutely gorgeous. Thank you." She held her breath, afraid to say any more.

"I'm glad you liked it. Look, Belle, I wasn't going to call. I figured that, for whatever reason, you'd made up your mind against me and I didn't have a chance of changing it."

"Russ, I'm sorry—I—"

"Wait. Let me finish. I tossed and turned all night, and finally came to the conclusion that I had to try one last time to convince you that I'm sincere in my desire to get to know you better. Belle, I think you're a lovely, talented woman, and I would be grateful if you'd agree to meet me for coffee this afternoon—just coffee and talk. Please?"

Belle smiled and felt the dark weight of despair vanish in an instant. Sometimes you did get a second chance at luck after all, she thought.

"I'd love to," she said quietly, and grinned at his whispered,

"Yes!"

"That's great," he said, and she could hear the smile in his words.

They made their plans, and Belle practically flew up the stairs to her bedroom to get ready.

COFFEE LED TO LUNCH and then dinner. That dinner led to many others. During the next couple of weeks, Belle and Russ found that they shared a great deal in common—chiefly, their mutual attraction.

Belle had never before been so happy or felt so beautiful and cherished. Feeling enlivened and filled with creativity, she started writing seriously and submitting her work with a vengeance, basking in Russ's unfailing support. In what seemed like the blink of an eye, the days turned into weeks and soon Christmas was just a few days away. Those wonderful days before the holidays became a whirlwind of Christmas shopping together, cozy lunches for two, and then private dinners where they began to open their hearts to one another.

ON CHRISTMAS EVE, Belle and Russ prepared to celebrate their first Christmas together. The smell of mulled wine and the fireplace greeted Belle as she entered the living room of Russ's house. He was waiting in front of the crackling fire with a mug of the spicy drink for them both. He lifted his mug to Belle's to toast.

"These weeks since I met you, Belle, have been the happiest time of my life. I am so glad my talented ladylove entered that jingle contest and brought us together. In honor of that, I've composed a little jingle of my own."

"Really? I can't wait to hear it."

He stepped closer and took her mug, setting both on the coffee table. Taking Belle's hands in his, he gave her a quick, soft kiss, looking intently into her eyes.

"It goes like this. *Belle's the one, from A to Z. I wonder if she'll marry me.*" He paused for effect and then said, "So, what do you think?"

He smiled at the obvious joy in her face and the happy tears brimming in her eyes. "I think your jingle just won first prize, Mr. Wakefield."

"And that prize is?"

She didn't answer with words, but her impassioned kiss told Russ all he needed to know.

Saint Nic

*N*icole Starr wrapped the scarf securely around her neck. Lower than normal temperatures were predicted for the day, with a 60 percent chance of snow. Nic wasn't taking any chances on catching a cold, not with her busiest season at hand.

"You look like a big elf," said the gangly teenager working the till at The Sugar Shack, Nicole's bakery.

"Maybe I do, Buffy, but at least I'll be warm," Nic shot back.

Nic smiled at her reflection in the mirror on the wall behind the counter. She did look rather like a large elf in her winter gear. The bright red knitted toque covered her dark brown curls, giving her a soft fringe that framed her round face. Her head was rescued from looking too small by the overly large green and red pompom that adorned the top of the hat. The red and green scarf was wound twice around her neck, hiding her slight double chin and giving the impression of a turtle about to retreat into its shell. Her long, navy wool cape was Nic's attempt to disguise a figure that reflected her ample gifts as a cook—a little rounder than she would have liked, but in the range still referred to as pleasingly plump. In concession to holiday spirit, under it she wore a red jogging suit appliquéd with holly and bells. An uncustomary dash of scarlet lipstick made her feel festive and daring.

She smiled. "Well, if this doesn't cheer them up, nothing will," she said.

"That hat will do it, for sure," Buffy teased.

"Hey, lay off the hat," Nic said with mock anger, "Mrs. Martin knitted it for me herself."

"Yeah? Well, Mrs. Martin is about 200 years old and can't see too well anymore. I'd say that hat is proof!"

"I don't pay you for the insults, kiddo," Nic shot back.

"No, those I give for free," Buffy laughed as a woolen mitten narrowly missed her head. "Are you coming back later?"

"No." Nic sighed. "I'm beat after the run we had this week. I'm due for a long soak in the tub and an early night."

The Sugar Shack had been doing a booming pre-Christmas business. The bell tinkled as another group of customers came into the store. "So, Saint Nic," one of the latest arrivals said, "looks ready to do her good deeds for the day."

Nic looked up and smiled at the husband of her best friend. "Oh, cut it out, Ted! I'm far from saintly," she said with genuine affection. "How did you manage to escape from the hardware store today?"

"Being the boss has its privileges," Ted said. "It's been a madhouse this last week. I had to get away from the mayhem for a bit and clear my head. I thought that one of your chocolate éclairs would be just the ticket."

"Oh, try my jumbo candy-cane macaroons instead," urged Nic. "Guaranteed to have you singing 'Jingle Bells' with the first mouthful. And I know what you mean by mayhem. I've been busier than the jolly man himself."

"You heard the boss, Buffy. One candy-cane macaroon to go." Ted pointed to a large wicker basket brimming with brightly colored aromatic packages. "Off to the hospital to spread holiday cheer, I see. Don't you ever stop?"

"Not often. It keeps me from getting into trouble," said Nic. "Is Lou on duty today?"

"I think she's on the pediatric floor," Ted replied. "Can't keep my sweet wife away from all those babies."

"You'd think she'd have her fill after your five." Nic laughed. She felt a small twinge inside despite her outer humor. She envied her friends' close marriage and happy family. Quickly shaking those thoughts from her mind, she reminded herself "what can't be helped must be endured," as her late father used to say.

"You're sure you can handle the shop for a couple of hours?" she said to Buffy as another customer entered the bakery.

"Are you kidding?" Buffy gave a dismissive wave of her hand. "Piece of cake, pardon the pun. Now, will you get out of here? I'm busy, you know."

Chuckling, Nic picked up the basket and was on her way, passing yet another couple headed into her shop. Nic always marveled at how a small farming town like Stanton could generate so many customers. Nobody seemed to do their own baking anymore. Not that Nic was complaining. All that revenue kept the roof over her head and the wolves at bay. And she was working at what she loved most in the world, creating sumptuous goodies to warm the heart and tempt the taste buds.

"Well, Saint Nic, have fun," Ted said, earning a swift elbow directed at his midriff. He opened the van door for Nic. "If you see my wife, remind her we have tickets to the concert at the town hall tonight."

"That's tonight?"

"You didn't forget, did you? You said you'd keep the monsters overnight so Lou and I can have a romantic evening on our own."

"Of course I didn't forget," Nic lied. So much for her quiet early night. "I just lost track of my days this week. No problem. Just drop the kids off at my place, say around six. If you like, I'll give them dinner, too. They love Auntie Nic's killer pizza."

"They love their Aunt Nic, period," Ted said with a warm smile. "It's because you spoil them."

"It's just because I don't have kids of my own," said Nic with only a tinge of regret in her voice. "I can afford to ruin yours a little bit."

"Gee, thanks," Ted said wryly. "See you later."

THE HOSPITAL was bustling with visitors. Nic was stopped numer-
ous times for visits with neighbors and customers. Her cheerful
voice and contagious laugh brought a smile to more than one bed-
ridden face.

One face in particular lit up considerably when Nic breezed
into her room.

"Hi, Mrs. Martin. How are you feeling today?" Nic perched
on the edge of the bed and took the frail hand of the tiny woman
lying there in hers.

"I'm fine, dear." Mrs. Martin's voice was wavery and thin, but
her eyes crackled with intelligence and good humor. She'd known
Nic since she was born. "Don't you look pretty in your Christmas
colors?"

Nic offered a warm, loving smile.

"Now, don't exaggerate, Mrs. Martin. Warm, yes; pretty? That's
stretching it."

"Nonsense," wheezed the old woman. "You're as pretty as a
picture and twice as nice. What's in your basket there?"

Nic had to grin at the enthusiastic childlike love of presents that
Mrs. Martin had. She approached each little package Nic brought
her with pure enjoyment.

"Well, you see," Nic said, pulling out a rather large, colorful
package from the basket. "Santa told me you'd been a particularly
good girl this year, and that I should deliver this in person to you."
Wafts of ginger floated up from the wrappings.

"You made my favorite!" Mrs. Martin said, tugging at the bow
and wrappings like a five-year-old on Christmas morning.

"I couldn't let Christmas go by without bringing you your favorite treat, now, could I?"

"You're such a sweet girl." The box opened to reveal cleverly
rendered gingerbread men complete with natty little icing waist-
coats and broad, grinning faces. "Aren't they the cutest!"

"And what's this?" The loud masculine voice filled with annoyance made both women jump.

"Nicole was just giving me my Christmas present," Mrs. Martin explained. "Nicole, this is Dr. Barkley. He's new here."

"How do you do, doctor." Nic extended her hand.

"Do you realize that my patient is a diabetic?" The anger he directed at Nic made her feel awkward and embarrassed.

"Yes, but—"

"And as such, she should not have sugary sweets?"

"Of course, but—"

"Are you so completely irresponsible that you would bring cookies to a diabetic?'

"Now just a minute—" Nic felt indignation rising in her chest. Who did he think he was?

"I think it best that you leave me to examine my patient—and kindly refrain from bringing her things she shouldn't have." With that cursory dismissal, he ushered her out and left her feeling stunned and angry, staring at the closed door.

"Of all the nerve!" Nic muttered. Outrage filled her, and the cheer of the day vanished in the indignity of the whole situation. To be so summarily trounced on by a stranger without even the courtesy of being allowed to defend herself. She had half a mind to storm back into the room and give the arrogant Dr. Barkley a piece of her mind, but she didn't want to upset Mrs. Martin any further. Instead, she stormed off to the elevator, intent on finding her friend Lou and venting her anger.

Ted was right. Nic found her deep in paperwork at the nurse's station on the pediatric floor.

"Wow, what's got you in a snit?" Lou said, seeing the anger blazing on Nic's face.

"Do you know that new doctor? Dr. Barkley?"

"Evan?" Lou was puzzled. Nic was bristling with outrage—and that was really rare for her. "He's a nice guy. What about him?"

"Nice guy!" Nic snorted her distain. "He's an arrogant, rude, obnoxious jerk!"

"What?" Lou's confusion was evident.

"He's completely full of himself and definitely on a major power trip!"

"Evan?" Lou shook her head. "You must mean someone else. Tall, terribly good looking, about 35, killer blue eyes—"

"That's him," Nic cut in. "Completely full of himself!"

"What happened?" Lou took Nic's basket and directed her to a chair.

"He just kicked me out of Mrs. Martin's room after reading me the riot act about bringing cookies to a diabetic!"

"But you always bring Mrs. Martin your special sugar-free treats. Didn't you tell him that?'

"Hah! He wouldn't let me get a word in edgewise, Lou. He was too busy being pompous and kicking me out. I'm so mad right now I could spit nails!"

"That just doesn't sound like Evan. He's such a friendly sort— and so popular with the patients, especially the older ones. He's very kind and gentle with them."

"You could have fooled me!" Nic gestured to her basket, "Look, I'm hardly in the mood now to deliver the rest of these. Could you maybe ask one of the volunteers to finish the job? They're all labeled. I need to go home and cool off before you drop the monsters off. Oh, by the way, your hubby wanted me to remind you of your date."

"Oh, I can't wait!" Lou's face lit up at the mention of her husband, and Nic felt that twinge of envy again.

"You two are like a couple of high school kids," she teased.

"Isn't it great?" Lou sighed. "I still get weak-kneed when he comes in the door. We have to get you hooked up, girlfriend."

"Hey, I'm an independent businesswoman," Nic said with a bravado she didn't feel. "Why mess with a good thing? Besides, Stanton isn't exactly brimming with eligible sorts. I think you tagged the last good one."

By six, Nic had calmed down and was truly delighted at the arrival of Ted and Louise's five adorable children.

"Auntie Nic!" They yelled in chorus as the five, ranging in age from twelve to three-and-a-half, vied with each other for her undivided attention.

Supper was a circus of squabbling, showing off, storytelling and endless questions. Nic's cheeks were flushed pink from the energy and joy of watching the kids while trying to meet the demands of pleasing each one. When the doorbell rang it was a welcome interruption.

Leaving the kids to wreak havoc on the Dutch chocolate cake and ice cream, Nic ran to answer the door and was stunned to find Evan Barkley on the other side. "What do you want?"

"I don't blame you for being angry with me," he responded quietly. "May I have a moment of your time?"

Nic stepped back, allowing him into the front hallway. "How did you know where I lived?"

"Mrs. Martin told me."

Nic noticed that he really *was* quite attractive. Why this should bother her, she didn't know.

"That was after she tore a strip off me for being so rude to you. She explained what a saint you are and how kind you've been to her and so many other older folks. She insisted that I come directly over here to apologize. Please—Nicole, isn't it? Please, accept my apology."

"Accepted," Nic said grudgingly. "But let me just say, you were way out of line. I would never do anything to harm anyone, especially Mrs. Martin. I'm clever enough to know that diabetics can't have sugar. I own a bakery, Dr. Barkley. I've done my research and have a specialty line of dietetic treats especially designed for customers like Mrs. Martin."

"I realize that now." Gone was the arrogant and self-assured doctor of earlier in the day. This was a humbled and penitent man. "Again, I'm sorry, and I'd like to make it up to you if I may and—"

A loud wail interrupted him and Lisa, Ted and Louise's six year old, came running from the kitchen. Tears streamed down her face, and when Nic picked her up to comfort her, she buried her head in Nic's shoulder.

"I'm sorry, Dr. Barkley, but I should see what this is about." Nic couldn't be sure, but she thought she saw a look of disappointment cross his face.

"Of course," he said quickly. "I didn't realize you had a family. I'll be on my way. Goodnight."

And he was gone before Nic was able to tell him that the children weren't hers.

The next week saw Christmas come and go and New Year's begin its approach. Nic was filled with the post-holiday blues. Things had slowed at the bakery and Nic was able to handle things, allowing Buffy an occasional day off. One day Louise noticed her friend's mood.

"How come so glum, chum?" Her stab at humor landed like a lead balloon. "Come on, talk to me. What's up?"

"Oh, Lou," Nic sighed. "It's the usual. Here we are with another New Year's upon us and I'm without a date for New Year's Eve. And for that matter, no prospects, either." She gave a mirthless laugh as she threw her hands into the air and shook her head. "I'm in a rut and I feel like I'm never going to get out of it. What's the matter with me?"

Lou put her arm around her friend and hugged her. They'd had this talk before. Lou knew that Nic sometimes envied her happy family life. "You have a successful business, Nic. And don't forget the friends and customers who love you. There's not one thing wrong with you."

"I know." Nic hugged her friend back. "But it just doesn't seem to be enough anymore." She straightened and started to bustle around the shop. "Oh, don't listen to me," she said, waving her hand in a dismissive fashion. "It's just the holidays talking. I'll be fine in a few days."

But Lou left The Sugar Shack with the germ of an idea formulating in her mind.

It was New Year's Eve and Nic had just brought out a pan of biscuits fresh from the oven when the tinkle of the bell alerted her to a customer's arrival. She looked up and was stunned to find Evan Barkley standing at the counter.

"They look good," he said, indicating the steaming biscuits

Nic still held.

"My grandmother's no-fail tea biscuits. Everyone seems to love them. In fact, my customers say these are the fluffiest tea biscuits they've ever eaten. And I have to admit, I do believe they are!" Flustered, Nic knew she was babbling. *Now the man must think I'm a complete idiot!*

"I've heard that The Sugar Shack is the best bakery around," he said, looking equally uncomfortable with the conversation.

"It's the only bakery around," Nic said, with a stab at humor. "But all modesty aside, I think it is the best."

Evan laughed, and the sound sent a thrill through Nic. His whole face was transformed. He really did seem pleasant. Nic began to relax a bit.

The bell tinkled, and in walked Louise. "Hey, Nic. The monsters demanded Auntie Nic's apple crisp for dessert tonight. Do you have one left?" She turned to Evan. "Oh, hi, Evan. I see you found The Sugar Shack."

"Sure did." Evan smiled. "I was just trying to decide which delicacies to indulge in." Turning back to Nic, he missed Louise's elevated eyebrows and knowing smirk. Nic blushed at the implication that she might be one of the delicacies to be considered. "Louise here has been singing your praises, I'm afraid."

"Oh, she has, has she?" Nic shot a murderous look in Louise's direction.

"Well, Evan is a poor bachelor," Louise said pointedly. "I was sure he couldn't be eating right. I remember what Ted was like before I saved him, so I just told him where he could find some of the best baked goods in town."

"That's nice of you," Nic said through gritted teeth. It was becoming clear that Lou was in matchmaker mode.

"Say, Ted and I had such a good time on our date last week," Lou said, continuing to ignore Nic's obvious discomfort, "that we'd like to do it again. Can you babysit the monsters for us again this weekend?"

"Baby-sit?" Evan looked puzzled.

"My hubby and I are the proud parents of five kids under the age of thirteen," Louise explained with a laugh. "We love them, but I must say we do look forward to a night off now and again. My single friend here," she nodded towards Nic, "kindly manages the herd for us when we go out. Auntie Nic is their favorite babysitter. Taking on my brood is definitely one of the reasons she's called Saint Nic." Louise smiled broadly. "So can you, Nic?"

"Aw, they're great kids, Lou. Sure, I'll watch them," Nic said, feeling a blush creeping into her cheeks.

"So you mean that wasn't your daughter?" Evan blurted, an element of hope in his words.

"Sadly, no," Nic said, catching the sly grin on Louise's face. She'd told Louise of Evan's visit the last night she babysat, and realized that Louise must have been orchestrating behind the scenes to bring the two singles together.

"Well, if you can get that apple crisp for me, I must fly," Louise chirped, looking happily from Evan to Nic. Nic could have kicked her at the moment, but smiled instead and rang up the sale. When Louise left, the two stood awkwardly looking at each other for a few moments.

"That night I came to your house to apologize," Evan said, clearing his throat nervously, "I assumed the little girl was yours."

"You left before I could explain," Nic said. "Just like I couldn't explain about Mrs. Martin."

Evan grinned sheepishly. "It seems I've made a habit of jumping the gun with you."

"A little." Nic couldn't resist one last dig, but she tempered it with a hearty chuckle.

"I came that night to offer to make it up to you for my rudeness by taking you out to dinner."

"You did?"

"Uh-huh. And when I saw the child, I assumed you were married, so I didn't ask."

"Oh?"

"Now that I know the truth, do you suppose I could persuade you to have dinner with me tonight?"

Nic's heart beat a rapid tattoo as excitement filled her. It didn't take her long to reply. "I'd love to." She worked to restrain herself from bubbling over with a gleeful shout.

"And if you like, I'd be happy to help mind the troops with you this weekend. That's if you don't have any other plans, of course."

Nic was thrilled by the look of hope on his face. "No plans. I'd love the help." She took a tea biscuit from the tray and held it out to Even with a bright smile. "Biscuit?"

Returning her smile, Evan reached for the biscuit and allowed his hand to linger on Nic's. The air seemed to hold a magnetic charge as the two just stood there holding that biscuit and grinning at each other.

Peeking through the window, Louise was delighted to see that a match had been made after all. Saint Nic and the doctor. Oh yes, it looked like the New Year held great promise.

Beyond Reason

*R*ita stood tensely at the entrance of the auditorium and surveyed the scene. The psychic fair hummed with activity, each colorful, festooned booth thriving with business.

To her dismay, the place was crowded. She hated crowds. Crowds made her feel extra conscious of her fuller curves, hips that seemed to bump into everyone, breasts that seemed to precede her through the space. But she should have expected this. Weren't psychics the rage at the moment? No doubt each person hoped to find the answers to life's questions.

Inexplicably, her breath caught in her chest. Why was she here, anyway? She didn't really believe in this stuff. She was practical, both feet firmly planted on the ground of reality. Perhaps it was seeing yet another friend get married a few days earlier and being reminded that she was in her thirty-fifth year, still alone. Or perhaps it was the well-meaning advice of her Mother to have more realistic standards where men were concerned—find a man who would date her despite her weight. Thanks, Mom, but no thanks! Perhaps it was just that she was lonely and had been celibate far too long and if she didn't use it soon, she'd lose it! But Rita knew none of these were the reason. It was the dream. The recurring, disturbing dream.

It always began the same way, a swirling of soft, billowing

smoke, eerie, oddly arousing music, and him. He was tall, ruggedly built, walking with a panther's awareness. Long, black hair billowed around his shoulders and down his back. Tight leather pants outlined muscular buttocks and an enticing generous bulge at his crotch. Rita blushed at the remembered vision. His shirtless chest was smooth, glistening in the obscure light. But when she looked up to his face, strangely, she couldn't see it clearly. Dark shadows cast by his mane of hair hindered her view. She had the impression of glittering dark pools for eyes.

As he came closer to her, his arms reached out. Large, long-fingered hands gestured for her to meet him. She felt herself drawn into his embrace. His warmth surrounded her. He caressed her back and hip while she inhaled the spicy fragrance of his skin. Hot breath hit her neck as he leaned over to nibble on her earlobe. Ripples of sensation coursed through her pliant body. Her eyes closed in rapture as his strong, full lips engulfed hers in a long, sensuous kiss. His tongue played tentatively against her mouth, teasing her lips open, allowing him entrance. Shyly, she sent her tongue up to meet his, where they thrust and parried with each other. Moments seemed like eons, when at last the kiss ended.

He ran his hands over her full breasts, teasing the peaks with his thumbs. His hands pulled her close against his obviously aroused body. She could feel the steel hard length of him bruising her pelvis. Desire mounted. She in turn stroked his hot skin and massaged his powerful muscles. A groan of response rumbled from him and he pulled her tighter.

It was always at this point that she woke up, panting, aroused and frustrated. Night after night the dream came to taunt her, never allowing her to follow the interlude to its obvious and desired conclusion. And it was for this reason that she had come to the psychic fair after seeing it advertised in the paper.

A sigh escaped from somewhere deep within her soul. This seemed like such a ridiculous thing to do. Did she really expect that some "medium" with dubious skills of seeing beyond the mortal pale could actually help her? Suddenly she felt quite ridiculous.

She was on the verge of turning to leave when her eye caught a fleeting glimpse of a man across the room, a strangely familiar man. Her heart thumped painfully. It couldn't be! She could only see his back, but there was the long, thick black hair, and the tall, well-muscled frame. Here?

Trance-like, she started across the room. He ended his conversation and moved away with long, loping strides. She hurried to keep up, following and trying to close the gap. Was it her imagination, or did he pause from time to time to allow her to gain on him?

Abruptly he stopped and turned into one of the booths. Seconds later she stood at the entrance of the booth, trying to calm her racing heart, her mind whirling at the possibility that her dream had come true. She entered.

The man was seated on the far side of a round table, facing the entrance. Subdued blue-tinted lighting made Rita want to whisper as if in church. The man smiled.

"Welcome. Please have a seat." His voice was deep and resonant, sending shivers down her spine.

"Thank you," she said softly, almost afraid to look at him now that she was here. She shrugged off her coat and sat demurely, a faint blush tingeing her cheeks. Lord, what was happening to her? She finally looked at his face. Her first glance took in high cheekbones, a clear wide brow, and the even white teeth framed by his smile. His eyes were hidden behind tinted glasses, much to her regret.

"I am Jordan Eaglefeather," he began. "You are here to seek answers. I am here to offer some. How can I help you?"

Now that the question was posed to her, Rita didn't know how to answer. It seemed so trite to say, "Please help me find the man of my dreams."

"Um—" God, she sounded like an idiot! "I've been having these dreams."

"Yes?" His smile was warm and inviting.

She found herself fascinated with his teeth. They were so white, so even. She stared, mesmerized. He was so handsome it unnerved her. She shivered slightly. Her eyes seemed to lose their focus. Everything took on fuzzy edges. Sound from outside the booth became muffled. A light buzzing filled her ears. Her head began to float as if separated from her body. She was having trouble concentrating on his words. She strained to hear him.

"Tell me about them," he prompted.

"Look, I'm wasting both our times here. I'm sorry. I'll go now." Rita stood and began putting on her coat.

"Rita," he said softly. "Sit down."

She sat abruptly, one arm in her coat. "How did you know my name?"

"Don't you know, Rita?"

She looked at him, puzzled. Wordlessly, he stood and walked around the table. Helping her to her feet, he gently took her coat and cast it aside. With quiet strength, he ran his hands down her arms.

"Don't you know, lovely Rita? Think long and hard."

Shaken, she looked up at his face. Seemingly on their own, her hands lifted to the dark glasses. She hesitated only a moment before removing them from his face. Deep, dark pools of liquid fire burned into her eyes. She was lost in the depth of his gaze. Her lips were drawn magnetically to his.

The kiss was ardent, full of promise and fire. His tongue teased her lips open to plunge deeply into her mouth, drawing every ounce of breath from her body. He pulled her close and she found her arms wrapping around him, pulling him closer and closer. Running her hands down his muscular back, she boldly cupped his buttocks, pulling his pelvis against her. She could feel the steely length of his arousal and suddenly she knew. She gasped and pulled back.

"It's you!" she whispered, her eyes wide with fear and smoky with desire.

"Yes, it's me, Rita."

"But how?"

"Does it matter?"

For a moment the fear battled with desire, and then desire won.

"God, no!" She threw herself into his arms, locking her mouth on his. Her fevered hands began to work at his clothing, loosening, removing, hungry for the feel of his skin.

His smooth, bare chest was hot to the touch. She feathered kisses across his chest, feeling his dark nubs tighten at her touch. His hands worked equally hard to rid her of the encumbrance of clothing.

The only sound in the room was the rasping of their breath in some lustful harmony. It was all so familiar, so real! Leaning into him, she slid her hand down along his belly to the waistband of his jeans. She heard his gasp as she deftly undid the button.

"I must know at last," she whispered. "Please, I must know."

Time blurred for Rita as they came together in a frenzy of lustful abandon. She gloried in the sensations created by this dream lover at last. Their clothes seemed to magically vanish, piece by piece, until they stood together in their natural state, skin against skin.

"Not here," he murmured. Taking her hand, he led her to a beaded curtain she had not noticed before. He swept the curtain aside and drew her into a room made for a lover's tryst. An enormous round bed dominated the circular space. A canopy of frothy tissue-thin cloth waved in the gentle breeze coming from several high windows around the room. A glimpse showed Rita a view of rolling green hills and deep azure blue skies, viewed as if from a high tower.

"How is this possible?"

"How can you ask that?"

Then all questions were forgotten as this glorious man took her into his arms and led her to the bed. The infinite tenderness he showed was everything and more than Rita had ever imagined.

He touched her like a blind man exploring new territory. He sampled her as he would any new delight, with relish and enjoyment. He would pause here and there, with special emphasis. First her face and throat, then her full breasts, her belly, her thighs. Each touch sent currents of electricity coursing through her body. She was lost in a stunning array of sensations.

She had never before known that love could be so magical, so pure, so perfect. She knew she was beyond reason. Her only thought was to reach fulfillment. As if understanding her need, he became more demanding, forcing responses from her that she had not known possible. As her moans and sighs increased, so did his attentions, until with a cry of joy, she reached the ultimate peak in harmony with him.

Rita was stunned by the force of her response to him. Never before had she experienced anything so primal. She rested in his arms and felt his tiny kisses on her neck and shoulders.

He eased back. With a final gentle kiss, he stood and spoke to the nearly unconscious Rita.

"Rest, my beauty, for I wish to show you the many other ways I will worship your body. I will make all your dreams come true. It is why I brought you here."

With those words, Rita felt darkness descending upon her. She drifted into a dreamless, restful world, conscious only of a floating sense of unreality. Perhaps she slept.

"Miss?" The deep voice penetrated her foggy state. "Miss, are you all right?"

Rita opened her eyes and found herself staring into a pair of deeply concerned green eyes.

"What happened?" she asked, embarrassed to have somehow lost contact with the moment.

Jordan Eaglefeather smiled. "Well, you came into my booth a few minutes ago. You sat down. I asked how I could help you, and then you went rather blank. Where were you?"

Rita blushed scarlet, remembering the intense sexual experience she had just imagined with this man. She continued to study his wonderful face. She was certain that he was the man from her dreams, yet reason told her it could not be possible. But this was beyond reason, for here he was in the flesh, not inches away from her.

Fear struck. Perhaps she was having a breakdown. Can loneliness drive you to mental frailty?

"Oh my God!" Rita scrambled to her feet, grabbing her coat and bag and running. Running from what, she wondered. Running from herself.

"Wait—" she heard Jordan's voice call. But she kept running.

FINALLY SAFE in the sanctuary of her tiny apartment, Rita worked to calm herself. It had been a mistake to go there. She was letting loneliness and an overactive imagination get the best of her. It was nonsense! Foolishness! She needed to stop this romantic silliness and get back to the practical work of living.

Exhausted from the afternoon, she decided a nap was in order.

Almost immediately, she was aware of being transported to the tower room of her earlier tryst. It was close to nightfall. Candles cast a soft, romantic glow. Rita awoke to find herself sprawled across the circular bed from her "episode." She was naked and could still feel the tingly afterglow of her lover's touch.

"So you're awake," said that delicious voice from somewhere behind her. She felt the bed give as her dream lover slid across to her. Strong, deeply tanned arms encircled her waist, and hands caressed their way up to cup her full breasts. She was instantly on fire.

"So beautiful," he murmured into her hair. "So passionate. So ripe."

She turned and stared at him. "Who are you?" she whispered, almost afraid to hear his reply.

It was his turn to stare at her. He seemed to be weighing his potential response to her question. His eyes softened. He smiled warmly, reassuringly. He gently brushed his fingers across her forehead and down her cheek. She shuddered at the pleasure of his touch.

"You know who I am, don't you?" he said, his voice a sensual caress. She found herself lost again in a hot, sweet kiss. And she knew.

"Yes," she breathed, before giving in to the frenzied needs that drove them both.

IT WAS A DIFFERENT RITA who arrived at the psychic fair later that day. The crowds had dissipated and some of the vendors and psychics were busy closing up shop. Had she missed him? No, somehow she knew he was still there, waiting. It didn't take long to arrive at his booth. All was quiet. Rita took a deep breath and entered.

The same blue soft light filled the space. Eerie, barely discernible music played. And Jordan Eaglefeather stood waiting.

Without a word, she walked into his embrace. Their lips met in a searing kiss, and all the remaining doubts in Rita's mind were vanquished.

"But how is it possible?" she cried. "You are a dream!"

"It's not me who is the dream, Rita," he replied. "You have been coming to me all my adult life."

Rita's astonishment must have registered on her face.

He continued earnestly. "I've traveled the dreamscape every night to visit you. We embrace and kiss passionately, both of us aroused and hungry."

He had unconsciously begun to stroke the skin on her bare arms. He could hear her breathing quicken. "I pull you in my arms to show you my passion, but the dream always ends there. I wake up, pulsing with the reminder of the interruption. I go almost mad with wanting you."

She was now running her hands over his shoulders and chest.

"I've wanted you to find me. Now you're here, and we're awake, and—" with that he pulled her to him, placing his lips close to hers. "—nothing can stop us."

He devoured her mouth, sucking her tongue into his mouth. She moaned and attacked his tongue with equal vigor. The kiss was deep, possessive, almost violent. Each fought to dominate the other, to be the victor in this sexual battle. And then Jordan abruptly pulled away and stood. With a seductive smile and with maddening slowness, he ran his hand down her body from shoulder to hip. She looked at him and smiled knowingly.

"It's time to fulfill both our dreams, lovely Rita," he said huskily. She opened her mouth to reply, only to find that his covered it in another mind-numbing kiss.

She knew then that she wouldn't wake this time. In finding Jordan Eaglefeather, her dreams had come true.

Once More— with Feeling

His voice was like dark chocolate truffle—smooth and silky. Carrie felt it coming over the phone line like a caress. She reached up to smooth the loose tendrils of slightly graying hair back into her ponytail and then abruptly stopped herself, feeling foolish for the gesture.

"Excuse me, but could you repeat that?" She held her breath waiting for his response. She heard his soft chuckle, as if he knew his effect on her.

"I talked to you yesterday about the apartment for rent," he said. "I'm interested in seeing it."

"Oh, yes, of course," she said, her tongue feeling thick and clumsy. The slight Southern flavor she detected in his speech only added to the appeal. "Please pardon me. I guess I'm a little distracted."

"No problem," he said. "Is this a bad time, or can I come around and see the place?"

"What? Now?" She cringed at how simple she sounded. How could the voice of a perfect stranger be rattling her normally cool, efficient self to such a degree? God help her, but she almost felt a giggle coming on.

"That would be great, if it wouldn't be too much trouble," said Mr. Velvet Tones.

Carrie cleared her throat and clutched at her composure. "Of course—ah, Mr.—" What had he said his name was?

"Donovan—Brent Donovan."

"Of course, Mr. Donovan. Can you find us all right?"

"Think so. I take a right at Spruce—"

"Yes, and then a left at the next street—Cypress—we're number 172."

"Thanks. See you in about twenty minutes or so."

Carrie stood for a moment after the call ended and took some deep, calming breaths. A picture of a tall, dark and devastatingly handsome man formed in her mind, and she paused to enjoy the vision. She flushed as she fantasized for a moment that she could walk into her vision's arms—nice, strong, protective arms—

"Who was it?" The raspy voice of her father broke into her pleasant reverie, and she felt a stab of irritation that she quickly squelched.

"Just someone about the apartment over the garage, Daddy," she said in a pleasant tone. But her face belied that tone.

"Where's my lunch?" he demanded in his quavering voice.

"Coming right away, Daddy," she said in response, and moved with weary steps toward the kitchen.

"It's past my lunchtime," he said again, sounding like a petulant child.

"I said, it's coming," she snapped, and immediately regretted her pique. He couldn't help it that he was old and ill. He was entitled to be cranky, she told herself.

She entered the converted sunroom carrying a tray on which rested her father's lunch: tomato soup, a grilled cheese sandwich and a glass of milk spiked with a little rum. It was the same every day. She had tried to entice him with a variety of tasty and tempting meals, for she was an accomplished chef, but he always wanted the same lunch day after day.

"Here we are," she said in a cheerful singsong and deposited the tray on a swing arm table by the bed. She bustled around to puff up his pillows and adjust him to a more upright position. "It's a lovely day today. I'll just pull open the blinds and let in some of the sunshine. It'll cheer you right up—"

"Don't want no sun heating up my room," her father said.

"Nonsense." She ignored his rudeness. "You can look over the gardens you worked so hard over the years to create and see the hundreds of birds that come to visit them." She swung the table over the bed and handed him his soup spoon. "Now you eat up like a good boy, and I'll just go let in the light."

Her father's critical words stopped while he slurped at his soup. Carrie opened the blinds and felt the warmth of the spring sun kiss her skin. She cranked open a window just a little to let in the fresh, crisp air. Leaning against the windowsill for a moment, she breathed in the fragrance of the mock orange bush that grew just below the window. The cool air felt good on her skin, and the happy sounds of chirping birds lifted her heart just a little.

"There," she said, plastering an overly bright smile on her face. Bustling about the room, she began to tidy. "What would you like to do this afternoon while I show Mr. Donovan the apartment? Would you like to watch a little television? Or shall I get the newspaper for you?"

"Nothin' but crap on the damn television, and more crap in the paper. Stop fussing," he said between bites of his sandwich. "I want you to read a bit more of that there book you started on last week."

"Moby Dick," she said, her irritation once again rising. "But Daddy, I can't. I have to show Mr. Donovan the apartment. He'll be here any minute. But it shouldn't take too long, and I'll read to you then."

"Hmmmph," he said, taking a deep draught of his milk and rum. "Don't know why we need to be rentin' that place at all. Don't like having strangers around."

"I explained all that, Daddy," she said. "I had to quit my job to take care of you, and your Social Security just isn't bringing in enough to pay all the bills. If I can rent that apartment you built for—" Here she paused to swallow the lump that had risen suddenly to her throat. "—for Ted and me when we were first married, then we should be able to make ends meet without difficulty."

"Ted? Where's Ted, then," her father asked, not aware that he had stuck a knife in his daughter's heart.

"Ted's gone, Daddy, remember?" she said. "He left three years ago. I think he's in California somewhere."

"Oh yeah," her father mumbled. "Never shoulda married him. Took up with that floozie." He looked at her then and scrinched up his eyes. "Pretty floozie, though. Nice and skinny, but with those big—"

"Daddy, please!" Carrie crossed her arms over her own ample bosom and turned away to hide her welling tears.

"What?" the old man asked. "Oh stop being so sensitive. Just like your Mother. Always so—" He stopped and seemed to lose focus. Tears welled up in his rheumy eyes. He pushed the table away and turned his face into his pillow.

Carrie clasped a hand over her mouth to stifle the sob that threatened to burst out. She mourned her mother, who had died shortly after Carrie's divorce had gone through and she had moved back home to the comfort and support of her parents' home. No one knew that her mother had been ill for a long time and had kept that secret to herself. Carrie's father had been devastated and the very essence seemed to drain out of him. When he suffered his stroke, there was no question but that Carrie would accept the job of caring for him.

She silently lifted the tray from the table and carried it out of the room. Only when she was safely away and in the kitchen did she let the tears come and the sob escape. She held on to the edge of the counter and surrendered herself to the great gulping spasms that rolled through her body.

Dear God. Thirty-eight, fat, and alone, caring for her difficult and senile parent.

I was a young woman once, she thought. *I was pretty and vivacious—a real big, beautiful woman. I had a good job and hope for the future. And now what? What do I have? Worries. Sorrow. Loneliness.*

The doorbell rang and Carrie jumped. She ran to the half bath off the kitchen and inspected her tear-washed countenance. She quickly splashed cold water on her eyes and cheeks and blotted them dry. A quick comb through her hair and she was running to the door before the next ring. Out of breath, she opened the door.

And her breath stopped in her chest.

He was tall—impossibly tall, well over Carrie's own 5 foot 11. His hair was cut close to his scalp, and he sported a well-trimmed moustache and goatee giving his face a rakish air. His skin was the color of butterscotch, and it was hard for her to determine his age, but she guessed early forties. The broad smile he wore made Carrie's heart skip a beat. He was clean cut and dressed in crisp slacks, an open neck shirt and a leather jacket. A whiff of a spicy cologne tickled Carrie's nostrils, and she breathed in deeply finally.

"Miss Lester?" he said, thrusting out his large, well-manicured hand.

Carrie gulped and nodded, extending her own hand. How warm and solid his grip was. "Um—yes, Mr.—um—yes." Carrie felt her face flush. She cleared her throat and, with a self-conscious laugh, started again. "You'll have to excuse me, Mr. Donovan—"

"Brent."

"Of course—Brent—and I'm Carrie," she said, shaking his hand firmly this time. "You caught me just finishing with my father's lunch. I got in a bit of a rush."

"I'm sorry if—" he began.

"No, no, that's fine. Normally he's done long before now, but I got sidetracked this morning and got behind schedule. Now, shall we just go out and see the apartment?"

"Great. So it's above the garage, right?" The couple walked briskly around the side of the house and toward the back of the property.

"Yes, Daddy—my father built it for my husband and me when we were first married. We were still in college and couldn't afford much then. It really helped us out."

"Oh. Where do you live now?" Brent asked.

Carrie flushed and then answered crisply. "I live here now and care for my father. My husband—I'm divorced."

"Oh, I'm sorry—" Brent fell silent.

"No, that's all right," said Carrie. "It was a long time ago."

They arrived at the bottom of the stairs that led to the apartment above the garage. Brent smiled at her, and Carrie's heart skipped a beat. For a moment it seemed like he might say something more. But with another quick smile he proceeded up the stairs, leaving a totally flustered Carrie behind. She shook her head and hurried up the stairs after him.

"This is great," Brent said as he wandered around the large open space, touching furniture and inspecting the corners.

Carrie had to agree. It was a great little apartment.

Basically, her dad had left it a large, open-concept space with nooks devoted to the various living needs. Here was the living room nook, with its futon, leather chair and a small desk. There was the galley kitchen and dining nook with its canny use of space. The bedroom nook, with its comfy double bed, given the illusion of privacy by a gauzy curtain that hung from ceiling to floor beside the bed. The small bathroom with shower off of the bedroom. There were lots of windows around the space, giving it an airy feeling and making it appear larger than it was.

"This is just great," Brent said again. "It's exactly what I need."

"I know you told me you were finishing a book," Carrie said. "Why here?"

Brent sauntered over to a window and looked down over the gardens and back lawn. Carrie sensed that she had asked the wrong question.

"It's none of my business, I suppose," she said. "I'm sorry I asked."

Brent turned and gave a wan smile.

"No need to apologize, Carrie," he said. Carrie had the urge to comfort him and was startled at the urge. He turned and looked out the window again. "I needed a new place—a fresh start. You'll laugh at this—" He turned and smiled at her, shoving his hands in his pockets. "I opened a map, closed my eyes, and stuck my finger on the map. This was the town I hit. So, here I am."

"Really?" Carrie stared and then grinned. "How—inventive."

Brent let out a hearty laugh. It made Carrie smile. "You're very diplomatic. Most people would say I was nuts."

"Well, most people are a little nuts themselves," she said, meaning it. "So what's your book about?"

"Life," he said, beginning to restlessly move about the space again. "Love, betrayal, redemption, pain, joy—" Once again he laughed. "I'm sorry." He took a checkbook out of his jacket's inside pocket. "I want to reassure you that I can afford to pay the rent. In fact I'd like to pay six months in advance, if I may. Call it a token of good faith."

"You're taking it, then?" Carrie was thrilled, and it must have showed, for Brent grinned in return. Carrie flushed scarlet and began bustling about tidying things that didn't need tidying. "That's wonderful. If you'll stop into the house before you leave you can sign the lease and I'll give you keys. There's a food mart just down the street so you can stock up on groceries. You're welcome to use the laundry facilities in the house if you like. When will you move in?"

"Tonight, if that's all right. I have all my things in the van."

"Tonight. Good."

Brent stood by the door as they left and looked thoughtfully at Carrie. They stood gazing at one another without speaking for several heartbeats, and Carrie could feel his warmth. He tilted his head to one side, and then smiled gently. "I have a good feeling about this," he said.

Carrie grinned at his back as he descended the stairs. His good feeling was contagious, she thought.

"I DON'T TRUST that fella," Carrie's father said.

She was shaving him and stopped mid-stroke in surprise at his words. "Brent, you mean? Why not?" She rinsed the razor and bent to her task again.

"I just don't. You never know with his kind."

Carrie stopped once more and stared in disbelief. "His kind, Daddy? His kind? What are you getting at?"

"He's too slick," groused the old man.

"Slick? Brent? Really, Daddy." Carrie chuckled. "He's very nice."

"He's too tall," continued her father. Carrie just laughed some more. She felt good—light. She had Brent to thank for that. In the three weeks since he moved in, he had become a fixture in Carrie's life. A nice, attractive fixture, with a smile that made her heart flutter, and she didn't think he was too tall at all.

"Don't be silly, Daddy," she said, wiping the remnants of shaving cream from her father's face. "How can someone be too tall?"

"And he cheats at chess," he said, snatching the towel from Carrie's hand and roughly wiping it around his chin.

Carrie laughed again. "Really, Daddy. He doesn't cheat. You just don't play very well. Never have. *I* can beat you at chess, for goodness sake."

Her father looked up at her with a quizzical expression. "You've been awful chipper lately," he said. "And what did you do to your hair?"

Carrie lifted a self-conscious hand to her newly colored and trimmed coif. "Nothing much. I just felt like a change—a little sprucing up," she said, and busied herself with clearing up the shaving things.

"Humph," her father said. "You don't have some notions about that Donovan fellow, do you?"

Carrie froze. "Wha—what? Of course not. Really, Daddy, you're letting your imagination run away with you."

She fled before her father could conjecture some more, for he had come too close to the truth for comfort. In her haste to exit the room, she didn't notice she wasn't alone in the hallway until she had practically crashed into Brent.

"Whoa," he said, and put his hands on her shoulders to stop her.

"Brent," she said in a choked whisper. How much had he heard?

"You're in quite a hurry," he said, careful to keep his voice low. "Your Dad must be in quite a temper today."

"You could say that," she said, smoothing her shirt and squaring her shoulders. "Care for some coffee? I just made a fresh pot."

"Sure," he said, an unreadable expression on his face. "I came to talk to you, anyway."

Carrie set about getting mugs from the cupboard and pouring the coffee. "Oh, what about?"

"Well, that depends now, I guess."

Carrie carried the mugs to the table and went to the fridge for cream. "Depends on what?" she asked as she sat. "You're being awfully mysterious today."

"Am I?" said Brent. "I don't mean to be, but I did overhear your Dad a few minutes ago."

Carrie flushed. She grabbed her mug and tried to mask her discomfort by taking a sip of her coffee.

"Yes, it was quite interesting," he continued, taking his time to doctor his brew and stir it. "And I wasn't completely satisfied with your answer to his question."

Carrie's hands shook, and she was forced to set her mug down or spill the contents. She tucked her hands under her thighs and tried to compose her face. "Oh?" Not original, but it did buy a few seconds.

"Yes, so here's what I'd like to know," he said. He set down his spoon, folded his hands together on the tabletop and fixed his eyes on Carrie's. "Do you have some notions about me, Carrie?"

Carrie gulped. A million random thoughts careened through her brain, none of them coherent or helpful. Her breath was caught somewhere halfway between her throat and her stomach. She knew her cheeks burned with color and her eyes must have been wide, trapped as she was in the headlights of his forthrightness. For the life of her she could not make words come out of her mouth.

She watched him smile and casually pick up his mug to drink. He never took his eyes from her face.

"Perhaps I should tell you some of my own notions," he said. "You see, Carrie, I've had notions about you since the day I signed my lease."

"You have?" she said. Her voice cracked with strain.

"I have indeed," he said with a hint of laughter in his voice. "And I finally worked up the courage today to come and ask you out."

"You did?" Carrie couldn't believe her ears.

"I did. So, Carrie—and I love what you did with your hair, by the way. Very becoming—Will you first answer my question? Do you have notions about me, too?"

Carrie hesitated a moment, then in a whisper said, "Yes."

Brent smiled broadly. "Great. I hoped so. So, lovely Carrie, will you have dinner with me tonight?"

She looked at him—his open face, the twinkle in his eyes, the genuine pleasure in her response, his full-lipped smile—and she nodded.

"I'd love to," she said, not quite believing this was really happening.

"THIS IS A NICE PLACE. I've never been to Bandini's before," Carrie said as Brent held her chair for her.

The restaurant was small and intimate, high-end without being ostentatious.

"It is nice, isn't it? I'm glad." Brent said, sitting and taking a good look at his surroundings.

"Glad?" Carrie said. She looked up to catch Brent's grin. "Oh no," she said with a chuckle. "Let me guess. You opened up the phone book to restaurants, closed your eyes and pointed."

Brent held up his hands in mock surrender. "Guilty."

"Good grief," she said, shaking her head. "We could have ended up at Bob's Burger Barn."

"Ah, I wouldn't have minded," Brent said, looking at her earnestly. "It was really the company that was important anyway."

Suddenly Carrie was lost for words. She felt her cheeks grow hot, and she found it hard to look at the attractive man across from her.

"Carrie?" His warm, deep voice beckoned, and she raised her eyes to find his looking at her intently. "Tell me about you and your husband. What happened?"

She took in a deep breath, ready for the rush of emotion that usually came with mention of her failed marriage, but she was surprised. Suddenly she wanted to tell him all about it. She somehow knew he would understand.

"We were so young," she began, "still in college. We thought we knew everything."

"Didn't we all at that age," Brent said.

"I did, at any rate," she said. "My dad was a—difficult man to live with, demanding and judgmental. I always felt that I somehow didn't measure up."

"In what way?" Brent's gaze was intense.

Carrie paused a moment, reluctant to continue on this vein, but his quiet attentiveness encouraged her to plunge on.

"I've always been a—a big girl," she said in a soft voice. "My mom was so slim and pretty. I always got the feeling that Dad was somewhat disappointed in how I looked." She held up a hand to stop Brent as he started to speak. "I know. I know. It's silly, but to a young, hypersensitive girl, very real. Mom was wonderful, though. She worked hard to be supportive and loving, and in my teens I seemed to hit my stride. I had some great friends in high school, and discovered that I enjoyed holding center stage. I guess you could say I was a bit of a ham."

Brent chuckled. "I bet you were a real cutie."

"I don't know about that," she said, "but I was popular and vivacious. I met Ted my last year of high school. He was my first real boyfriend, and I figured I had met the love of my life."

"And you didn't?"

"Well, what does one know at seventeen and eighteen?" Carrie looked up and gave a sad smile. "It was so nice to feel normal and show my Dad that someone thought I was desirable."

Brent reached across the table and captured Carrie's hand in his. "You are, Carrie."

Carrie was struck dumb by Brent's words. She searched his eyes for the truth and saw the attraction to her there. It thrilled her and frightened her in equal measure. Stumbling over her words, she attempted to finish her story.

"Ted worked hard to build his accounting practice after college, and I started teaching kindergarten. I loved my job—my life, but I didn't notice that Ted wasn't as thrilled with it as I was. His business wasn't exactly flourishing right away, and he resented having to move into the apartment at my parent's. As I said, my dad could be difficult."

"Did your dad and your husband get along?"

Carrie's laugh had a bitter edge. "Hardly. It got so that they hardly spoke to one another. That at least was better than the constant arguing. I could feel Ted growing more distant, and I should have seen the signs of what was to come. We finally moved to another city and things were better for a while. Ted's business finally grew to a respectable volume, but he was restless, and one day I stopped by his office to find him in *flagrante* with a client—a very pretty divorcee."

Brent squeezed her hand. "I'm so sorry, Carrie."

"It was awful. We had a huge fight and he said awful things. A few days later he moved out and that was that."

"He was a fool," Brent said.

"You're very sweet," Carrie said, swallowing the lump that had risen in her throat. "Thank you for listening. I haven't talked about all this in a long time."

"I'm glad you trusted me," he said. "There's been no one since?"

Carrie pulled her hand from under his, immediately missing the warmth of his skin. "Well, I moved home and nursed my broken heart for a while. Then I took care of my mom before she died, but then Dad had his stroke and I quit my job to nurse him. I guess I haven't really considered trying to find love again. I think in some ways I've come to believe that it's just not in the cards for me."

"Nonsense," Brent said, and stood abruptly. "Look, I notice that there's a little dance floor over by the keyboard player." For the first time Carrie noted the soft, romantic music that must have started while she was telling her life story. "Would you care to dance with me, Carrie?"

She hesitated, but then could not resist the chance of being held in Brent's strong arms, even for a few moments on a dance floor. She placed her hand in his offered one and followed him.

From the moment his arms went around her, Carrie was in heaven. They were a perfect fit. Brent pulled her close and held her hand clasped against his chest over his heart. Carrie's head rested perfectly at his shoulder. She was aware of how good he smelled. The scent was spicy, subtle and purely masculine. She felt his warm breath caress her temple, and a shiver of longing rippled through her.

"It feels good to hold a beautiful woman close," Brent murmured. "It's been a while."

"Beautiful?" Carrie looked at him, looking for mockery in his face and finding only sincerity. She heard his low rumble of laughter.

"Yes, beautiful," he said, smiling down at her. "Has no one ever said that to you before?"

Carrie let the music float over her as she thought of her answer. Had anyone? Early in their courtship, Ted had told her she was cute. Her mother told her she had a pretty face. Her dad? Well, her dad was more often thoughtless in his teasing remarks about her figure. But beautiful? No.

"No," she replied, not looking at Brent. "'Beautiful' is not a word I've heard often."

"Well, then, it seems it's about time," he said. He used his index finger on her chin to tilt her face up, so she was gazing into his fathomless brown eyes. "You're beautiful."

Her heart pounded, and it seemed to affect her hearing. The music and voices of the restaurant faded to a low hum and all she could hear was the beating of her pulse.

Brent smiled as if he knew the effect his words had on her. She wanted to pinch herself to test the reality of her being here with him in the romantic setting. They swayed to the music, and then his face was moving closer to her, his eyes intent on her mouth.

She closed her eyes. When she felt the soft press of his lips against hers, her bones became fluid and she was sure she would fall at his feet.

But she didn't. The gentle kiss was brief, leaving Carrie wanting more. Brent's arms tightened around her and they finished their dance.

The rest of the evening for Carrie was wrapped in a gauzy veil of wonderment. She and Brent talked through dinner, but she could not later recall the details of their conversation. She could, however, describe the warmth in his eyes, the way a dimple appeared in his left cheek whenever he smiled, how he laughed without restraint and listened intently when she talked.

When Brent signaled for the check, Carrie felt a surge of deep disappointment. She didn't want the night to end. The two walked hand in hand to Brent's car.

"Let's not go home just yet," he suggested.

"Okay." Carrie was beyond protesting. Her heart was beating a crazy tattoo and she felt light on her feet, like she was filled with feathers.

They drove in companionable silence to a park on the outskirts of town. The park was on the edge of a small lake, lit this night by an almost full moon. Other cars dotted the parking lot, and Carrie giggled.

"What's so funny?" Brent asked, smiling at her mirth.

"I was just thinking, it's been a very long time since I've gone parking with a boy."

He chuckled. "Well, I haven't taken a girl parking for a long time, either. Let's see if I remember how this goes." He leaned across the seat and gave her a quick, impassioned kiss that took her breath away. He sat back and watched her face.

"Well?"

She flashed him a shy smile. "I think you did just fine. But I may need a couple more just to be sure." This bit of teasing made him grin.

"Glad to oblige," and once again pressed his lips to hers. This time the kiss was not a quick peck but instead a lingering, gentle exploration of her lips.

Carrie had never been so affected by a kiss before. It was as if she was just discovering she had lips. She slid across the seat closer to him and reveled in the feel of his arms around her. He pulled her close until they pressed chest to chest.

The kiss deepened as his tongue urged her lips to part. She nearly melted as his tongue caressed hers, sending long forgotten sensations coursing through her body. She was on fire, and yet she shivered.

It was the intrusion of a flash of headlights entering the parking lot that pulled Carrie to her senses. She pulled from Brent's embrace and slid back to her own side of the seat.

"What's wrong?" Brent asked. His eyes glittered with passion and his lips were swollen from their shared kisses. He had taken on a disheveled air, and Carrie thought he had never looked sexier.

"Nothing," she said. Noting the concern on his face, she added, "Really. I guess I'm a little overwhelmed by tonight."

"I hope, though, that you're as happy as I am," said Brent, reaching out to push a tendril of hair off her cheek.

"Very happy," she said. "It's just been a long time for me and I—I need a little time to absorb it all."

"Fair enough," he said, starting the car. Then he turned and looked once again at her. "Just believe that I am truly attracted to you, and I see tonight as the beginning of something serious."

She couldn't find words to reply, so she just nodded.

It was very late when they pulled into the driveway. Brent walked her to the door of the main house.

"Thank you," she said, keeping her voice low so as not to wake her father. "I had a wonderful evening."

"So did I, beautiful," he said, running a finger down her cheek. "There will be many more." He bent his head and captured her mouth in a searing kiss that sapped all the strength from her body. It was only Brent's arms around her that kept her on her feet.

"Good night," he whispered, and walked away.

She followed him with her eyes until he disappeared into the shadows of the garage. A few moments later she saw the light come on in the apartment. Fighting the urge to run to his door, she turned and entered the dark house.

Her father was in a querulous mood the next morning.

"You were out mighty late last night," he said as she laid out his breakfast things.

"We went for a drive after dinner," she said, feeling a rush of heat in her face.

"Is that all?" her father said.

"Daddy!" She was embarrassed.

"Oh, don't be so prissy," the old man growled. "You chasin' after him?"

Carrie wanted to flee. She grabbed the tray and sped to the door, hoping to end the uncomfortable conversation.

"I was all alone, you know," her father's voice ground on.

The statement was so unfair. Mrs. MacDougall from next door had agreed to pop in and give her father his dinner and help him get ready for bed.

"I need you here, not chasin' after some slick character. What do you know about him? He'll turn out just like that useless husband of yours—mark my words. Have you no pride?"

Carrie fled the room without answering. Her eyes welled with tears. She slammed the tray onto the counter and gripped its edge so the tips of her fingers turned white. But despite her attempt to vent some anger at her unreasonable father's cruel words, fear swept over her. Could he be right?

Carrie realized she really didn't know much about Brent's life before he'd appeared on her doorstep. He'd said he needed a fresh start, but a fresh start from what? He's had enough money to pay six months' rent. Where had that come from? He was writing a book. Was it his first? What had he done before? Did he make a habit of making fresh starts, running when things got too complicated?

The sudden rush of uncertainty that flooded over Carrie forced her to sit at the kitchen table, which was where Brent found her minutes later. "Good morning, beautiful," he said, bending to plant a kiss on her cheek.

Carrie felt the kiss but didn't respond. Her mind whirled with conflicting emotions. Out of the corner of her eye she saw him sit, and she sensed his confusion.

"What's wrong?" he asked.

Carrie turned her face and looked at him, not speaking for several moments. "Tell me, Brent," she said, her voice low and tight.

"Why did you come here?"

"What? You know why. I stuck my finger into the map—"

"I know that," she snapped. "But why did you need to move?"

Brent frowned and shifted in his chair. Carrie's chest felt tight.

"It's not important, Carrie," he said. "What's important is what we've begun here together."

"No, no, it *is* important," she said, shaking her head. "Are you running away from something, Brent—in some kind of trouble? Are you a slick operator, like Daddy says? A few months from now, will you choose another spot on the map and leave?"

Brent visibly stiffened and his face went tight.

"Is that what you think, Carrie?" he said.

Carrie sighed. "No. Yes. Oh, I don't know. Daddy asked me what I knew about you, and I realized I know very little. He said you'd turn out like Ted and leave. Oh, I'm so confused." She put her head in her hands.

Brent stood. "You do know me, Carrie. I've been completely honest about my feelings. As to my past, well, it's painful. I wanted to leave it behind and start fresh—be happy again. But since it's so important to you to know, I was a lawyer. I had a wife and a baby son and a great house in the country. We were happy, I thought, until I discovered that my wife had been involved with my law partner from the time we were engaged. And if that wasn't enough pain, my son wasn't mine. So, Carrie, that's my story. I quit my practice, left the whole rotten mess behind, and came here. I'm writing a book hoping to exorcise all the demons. I never planned on meeting you, on losing my heart, but like a fool, I did."

"Brent—" she said, and then couldn't find the words.

"Open your eyes, Carrie. Your *Daddy* is a bitter, frightened old man," he said. "And scared to death of losing you. I can understand that. It's hard to get old and sick. But Carrie, he's wrong about you and me. We both deserve better than we got." He gave her a last look, then turned and left the house.

Carrie watched him go, wanting badly to chase after him, to apologize for her doubts, to wrap her arms around him and not let go. But she was afraid.

"Carrie!" Her father's call roused her, and she stood to go tend to him. She wiped a stray tear from her cheek and took a deep breath.

"Yes, Daddy?"

"I'm thirsty."

"I'll get you some ginger ale," she said, standing in thought by the door.

"Well?"

"In a minute, Daddy." She took a long look at the old man in the bed. He looked so small lying there, and he'd gotten thin. His hands shook all the time now, and he wore a perpetual frown. And looking into his eyes, she was astonished to realize that Brent was right. Her father was afraid, and for Carrie, that awareness made all the difference.

She ran down the hall and out the kitchen door. Taking two steps at a time, she bounded up to the apartment and pounded on the door. It seemed to take forever for Brent to answer, and when he did, Carrie threw her arms around him and kissed him soundly on the lips.

"Forgive me, Brent," she said, out of breath and euphoric. "I've been a damn fool, but I hope you can overlook it and give me another chance."

Brent's face broke into a grin and he wrapped his arms around her, pulling her close. "No problem," he said, and bent his head to capture her lips in a kiss that went on forever.

Carrie's senses were thoroughly scrambled when at last the kiss ended.

"What changed your mind?" He led her to the futon where they sat, arms wrapped around each other.

She smiled.

"I opened my eyes," she said, before lifting her face to claim his lips once more—with feeling.

Chance Encounter

*T*he phone rang and Karen jumped.

"Damn!" she said. Her hands shook so much that she dropped the hairbrush.

"Get a grip, Kay," she muttered. "It's only a date."

Only a date! Only the first one she'd had in eight months. Only the first one she'd ever instigated herself, thanks to a personal ad. Would they hit it off? Would he be a nice guy? Would he take one look at her and bolt for the door?

"Whoever you are, this better be important," she said, reaching for the phone. "Hello!"

"What's got your knickers in a knot?"

Karen relaxed at the sound of her best friend's voice. "Help!" she squeaked. A chuckle came back in response. "Seriously, Fran. Help! I'm just a big ball of anxiety."

"Relax, girlfriend," Fran drawled. "He's only a man, not a beast. Not that there's much difference."

"Great. I'm seeking advice from a card-carrying man-hater." Another chuckle rumbled over the line.

"I don't hate the poor things," Fran said. "I just don't take them very seriously any more. Unlike you, I'm not a hopeless romantic."

"But you've had more experience in the romance department than I have," Karen said, wondering if she should change into her black stockings. "After Roger, I don't trust my taste in men at all."

"Don't go by my track record," Fran said. "I've had more than my share of crash-and-burns. But I survived and so will you. Just relax and have a good time tonight."

"Easy for you to say," Karen said. "What if—"

"Stop right there! Don't 'what if' yourself into a nervous collapse. Have I taught you nothing? Say after me: 'I will have a good time.'"

"I will have a good time," Karen said, grimacing.

"Not exactly convincing, but it'll have to do," Fran said. "Call me when you get home. I want all the details."

"Not that there'll be any," Karen said. "But okay. Wish me luck."

"Luck!" With a click, the comfort of Fran was gone.

She could still vividly recall the ugly scene with Roger just eight months earlier. It had been a hard climb back to the point where she felt worthy of a man's attention again. And her grip on that point was tenuous at best.

They'd dated for twenty months and lived together for another three. Karen was still awed that someone like Roger had chosen her, even though he'd proven to be such a disappointment. Roger was tall, slim and attractive in a Marlboro Man sort of way—rugged good looks, her mother called them. Tall herself, Karen outweighed Roger by eighty pounds. If she could have seen past her weight she would have noticed that her wavy chestnut hair framed a clear-skinned face and her long, dark lashes enhanced bright green eyes.

Roger hadn't helped. He had a disturbing habit of using her size as a weapon, or as his own private joke. He said he was only teasing, but it hurt. It hurt like hell. But she loved him. She excused his meanness as just his way, even when her friends told her she was being a fool.

Their last fight started over a silly, innocent question from Karen about Roger's whereabouts one afternoon. He exploded, shocking her with those awful words. "As fat as you are, you should be grateful I'm even here at all." She pleaded with him to stop, but he only hurled more hurtful words.

Within days, she had packed and left. After an ocean of tears and many long months, she was able to smile again.

Determined to help Karen through the difficult transition, her friends comforted her and talked Karen into a complete makeover. She added highlights to brighten her already lovely hair and bought new clothes and makeup in fresh shades. She began to feel reborn.

That spring, a chance encounter brought another change. One soggy Saturday morning Karen dashed from her car to the mall entrance, trying to stay dry despite the sudden downpour. She hunkered under a newspaper and cursed herself for forgetting her umbrella. At the point she leapt over a large puddle right at the entrance, her forward foot hit muddy slime and she felt herself going down.

"Crap!" Her newspaper and dignity lost, she sat, winded, on the hard pavement. And then a strong, masculine hand reached down to help her back to her feet.

"Are you all right?" said a deep, concerned voice.

"I'll live," Karen said, wiping puddle from her legs. "I should have been—" She looked up into the warmest pair of dark brown eyes she'd ever seen. Below them was a generous mouth split into a wide, white smile.

"—watching where I was going, " she finished lamely.

"Well, if I'd known such a lovely lady would be falling at my feet, I would have been watching for you," he said, and chuckled.

Karen was momentarily rattled. *Me? Lovely?*

"Th-th-thank you," she stammered, rewarding him with a generous smile of her own.

"Not at all," he said. For a few frozen seconds their eyes connected, then with a cheery "take care, now," he hurried across the parking lot, leaving Karen to pick up her senses and get back to her errands.

For several days after she walked on a cloud, replaying his "lovely" comment over and over. *Lovely—lovely—lovely—*

She relived the moment many times in the months since. At unexpected moments his deep voice echoed in her mind. She could close her eyes and vividly recall the strong grip of large, capable hands, the generosity implicit in his wide smile, the hint of mischief in those deep, dark eyes.

The memory of the encounter left her breathless, as if she'd just climbed a steep flight of stairs. Then she'd laugh at herself for behaving so foolishly.

She'd dated a few guys in her post-Roger days. One was the co-worker she'd found interesting and who had been asking her out for years. Reality was far different from her fantasy. He reminded her far too much of her ex. There'd been the inevitable set-ups by her friends, those blind dates that people dread. One or two had been okay, but on the whole Karen found the guys dull and self-absorbed.

WEEKS LATER, Karen and her friends Mary and Fran sat in a coffee shop after their weekly girls' night out.

"I think the personals are a great way to meet someone," Mary said. "You have complete control. You pick the ad or place one. No having to go to smoky bars or those awful single's dances."

"No more blind dates!" Karen said with a grin.

"All right," Mary said, "so we haven't exactly found you Mr. Right. I haven't given up yet."

"Spare me, please," Karen said. "I don't need the aggravation."

"Hey, you should place an ad, Karen," Fran suggested. "'Jaded female wishes to meet perfect man for lifelong bliss.'"

"I don't want a perfect man, but—"

"It's a great idea," Mary piped in. "We'll help you write it."

"Let you and Fran write an ad for me?" Karen raised her brows in disbelief. "Lord help me!"

"All right," Fran said. "We'll stay out of it. But you should think about it, really."

"I don't know," Karen said. "Isn't there a danger of meeting a lot of losers?

"Hey, you've got to kiss your share of toads before you meet a prince."

"Yeah, but who needs the warts?" Fran said. They all laughed, but the conversation planted a seed in Karen's mind.

Not long after, Karen was indulging her habit of reading her Sunday paper over a leisurely morning breakfast. The sun was warm on her back and she could hear birds chirping outside her window. A sense of wellbeing and contentment settled on her.

The memory of a pair of warm eyes and a brilliant smile drifted into her mind and she sighed. *Lovely—lovely—lovely—Oh, if only I'd been brave enough to say something to him—If only—*

With a shake of her head, she turned her attention back to her paper and found herself reading the personals.

SWM, early 30s, successful, movie star good looks. Seeking tall, slim model or actress to enjoy jet-set lifestyle.

Right! No ego there.

DBM, 42, blue collar worker. Seeks strong-minded woman. Let me be your love slave.

Ah, no thanks!

After skimming through the more outrageous ones, a small ad at the bottom caught her attention. She read and her heart began to beat a rapid tattoo.

SW nice guy, 35, looking for the lovely lady who fell at my feet in the rain. Your smile has lived in my heart.

Karen was stunned. She read the ad again. *Lovely—lovely—lovely.*

She set the paper down. She couldn't sit still. Her body quivered with an excess of energy. She attacked her household chores with a vengeance.

What should she do? She occasionally glanced at the newspaper and its provocative ad on the table. A sense of recklessness began to build inside her until, late in the afternoon, she threw caution to the wind and composed a short letter.

Dear Mr. Nice Guy,
Your smile has remained with me, also. Finding your ad today

*was wonderful. Responding to an ad is completely out of my
character, but I feel as if a part of me knows you already. Name
a place and time and I promise not to land in a heap at your
feet.*

Karen

Her hands were trembling when she mailed her response to
Mr. Nice Guy.

LIFE GOT BUSY over the next two weeks, but the ad and her letter
were never far from her thoughts. Then one afternoon a simple
white envelope appeared on her mailbox with unfamiliar writing
and no return address.

Her heart thumped erratically as she opened the letter and
read:

Dear Karen,
*Thank you for your note. Ever since our fateful meeting, your
loveliness has resonated in my mind. I finally found the courage to seek you, and I'm glad you read my ad and responded.
I go to the Java Café on Bond Street for coffee every evening
around 7. Let's meet.*

With anticipation,
Derek

She punched out Fran's number.

"Jeez Louise!" Fran said. "He really placed an ad looking for
you?"

"Yes," Karen said, "but what do I do now?"

"Are you kidding?" Karen felt Fran practically jumping through
the phone. "Go meet him!"

"But what if he doesn't like me?"

"So what?" was Fran's reply. "What's the worst that can happen? You don't hit it off. At least you tried, instead of sitting home
alone."

"True," Karen replied. "So you really think I should go?"

"What, do you want me to come and drag you to the café?"
Fran, in her own inimitable way, made Karen's decision.

IT TOOK KAREN THREE DAYS to work up the courage, but at last, curiosity won over timidity. Now here she was, moments away from leaving to meet him.

With a critical eye, she looked at herself. Not bad. Her hair fell in soft curls about her shoulders. Carefully applied makeup made her eyes appear huge and gave her skin a subtle blush. Her new dress in just the right shade of green flattered her voluptuous curves and made her feel totally feminine and pretty.

With a last smile to her reflection, she said, "Good luck, friend," and left for the café.

KAREN JOSTLED HER WAY through the wall of customers waiting to place their orders at the counter. She craned her neck, trying to find Derek in the sea of bodies. She experienced a moment of panic, wondering if she'd be able to find him. What if he hadn't come?

She broke through the congestion and, taking a deep, calming breath, began to scan the room. A man in the back sat with his head bent over a book. Could that be him? She made her way to the table. Warm brown eyes looked up at her, and the smile she remembered so well formed.

"It *is* you," she said.

"I certainly hope so," he said, his beautiful eyes sparkling with humor. He stood and cocked his head to one side, scanning Karen's form from head to toe. "This is my lucky day. It's my lovely rain-drenched lady. Hello, Karen."

She sat, and their eyes locked. *Pinch me,* Karen thought happily.

"I've been looking for you these past few days," Derek said. "I was afraid maybe you wouldn't come."

"It took awhile to find my courage," Karen said. "But I'm here now. I hope that's okay."

"Lovely," he said, and took her hand in his.

Yes, lovely, Karen thought, and smiled.

About the Author

*J*udy Bagshaw is a retired elementary school teacher and writer in Southern Ontario, Canada. As a plus-sized woman, she has long wanted to see stories featuring full-figured central characters. Much of her work features such characters leading rich and active lives, as she does.

Romantic suspense is her genre of choice, but she also writes humor, some non-fiction, and children's stories. Her currently available works include several novels, work in three anthologies, and a short story collection. She was also part of the writing team for the Ginn Reading Steps from Pearson Educational, a program widely used in elementary schools.

You can find out more about Judy, and read excerpts and reviews of her books, at www.judybagshaw.com.

She can be contacted at judy_bagshaw@yahoo.ca. Sign up for her fan newsletter at http://www.geocities.com/judybagshaw_fanclub/.

For news and updates about other Pearlsong Press books and authors, visit the Pearlsong Letter blog at
www.pearlsongpress.com
or subscribe to the free Pearlsong Letter e-mail newsletter at
www.pearlsong.com/subscribe.htm.